by John Hersey

*These are Borzoi Books
published in New York by Alfred A. Knopf.*

THE WALNUT DOOR

THE
WALNUT
DOOR

by John Hersey

 New York, Alfred A. Knopf, 1977

THIS IS A BORZOI BOOK
PUBLISHED BY ALFRED A. KNOPF, INC.

Grateful acknowledgment is made to the following for permission
to reprint previously published material:

April/Blackwood Music: Three lines of lyrics from the song
"Knocking Around the Zoo" by James Taylor (p. 81) reprinted
from the album entitled James Taylor. Copyright © 1971 by
Blackwood Music, Inc., and Country Road Music, Inc. All rights
reserved. Used by permission.

Galaxy Music Corp., N.Y., U.S. and Canadian Agents: Eight lines
of lyrics by Henry Purcell (p. 4) reprinted from Come Let Us
Drink, edited by Michael Hyman. Copyright © 1972 by Galliard
Ltd. All rights reserved. Used by permission.

Library of Congress Cataloging in Publication Data
Hersey, John Richard [date] The walnut door.
I. Title.
PZ3.H4385Wam3   PS3515.E7715   813'.5'2   77–1148
ISBN 0–394–41742–9

Manufactured in the United States of America

First Edition

For Margie and Dan Lang

THE WALNUT DOOR

Chapter 1

Movers carried in her things on the seventh of May. Elaine stood in the middle of the living room watching two strong guys heft the fragments of her tentative personality upstairs on their backs and in their arms.

Her brass-framed bed, her butcher's-block table, her little box of flat-bowled Chinese porcelain spoons. Her architectural drawing board. Her six terrariums. Her Cohasset Colonial rocking chair, which she had assembled herself from a kit. Her dulcimer—two strings missing. Her wok. Her big full photo album with her past stuck forever to the brown loose-leaf sheets with LePage's Mucilage.

She welcomed the need for a new album. The pictures were going to be all different in the new book. They were going to be snapshots of a person rocketing along in a straight line.

One of the movers, a disapproving black man, spoke not a word to her. The other seemed to think he was Elliott Gould with muscles.

"What's this?"

"An Appalachian dulcimer."

"Oooh, pahdonnay mwah."

He tucked the hourglass-shaped instrument under his arm like a banjo, strummed once, tuned the three surviving strings to intervals of fourths, and over tiny stainless-steel droplets of plinking sang with a sweet, trained voice:

Tenor:
>*"Since time so kind to us does prove,*
>>*So kind to us does prove,*
>*Do not, my dear, refuse my love."*

Falsetto:
>*"What do you mean? . . Oh fie! . . nay what do you do?*
>>*You're the strangest man that e'er I knew:*
>>>*I must . . I must . . . . I can't forbear,*
>>>>*I can't, I can't forbear."*

Tenor:
>>*"Lie still, lie still my dear."*

"You don't play it that way," she said. "You lay it on your knees."

He said, "I don't lay nothin from a kneelin position, modom."

His colleague said, "Move your ass, man."

All this simply passed over her as the shadow of a hawk's wing, too swift to chill. She hardly noticed; she was tightly collected, like a ball of twine, around the future.

Later Elliott Gould appeared in the doorway with a box of books. She half-turned away; she did not even want to look at that box. It was her carton of assorted false starts. *Utopia or Oblivion*, by Buckminster Fuller. *The Collected Stories*, by Flannery O'Connor. *The Human Use of Human Beings*, by Norbert Wiener. *How to Have a Green Thumb Without an Aching Back*, by Ruth Stout. *Middlemarch*, by George Eliot. *The I Hate to Cook Book*, by Peg Bracken. *Tristes Tropiques*, by Claude Lévi-Strauss. *A Modern Herbal*, by Mrs. M. Grieve, F.R.H.S. *Tao Te Ching*, by Lao Tzu. *Poems*, by Emily Dickinson. *Women and Their Bodies*, by the Boston Women's Health Collective. *The Future of Man*, by Pierre Teilhard de Chardin. *The Little Disturbances of Man*, by Grace Paley. *How to Get a Job Overseas*, by Curtis Casewit.

The black man just then was out in the truck. Elliott Gould stood inside the door holding the heavy carton, his bulging upper arms flushed with the pulse of lucrative work.

"I get through around four. Can I come over and play house?"

He wasn't bad-looking. Tee shirt with the sleeves cut off at the shoulder holes and with a picture of Janis Joplin peeking out now from behind the book box. Those roseate arms of his, she guessed, had just a few too many six-packs of Bud in them to qualify as Michelangelesque; maybe you could say they were of the school of Rubens. He knew what he was up to, she thought, cutting off those sleeves. Then she realized with a start that both Elliott Gould and Janis Joplin were staring at her breasts.

She crossed her arms. "Thanks, but no."

He shrugged, books and all. "No harm trying. Look, where do you want all this lineal communication?"

"Right there in the corner."

He put the books down and straightened up. "Strange town," he said, "wouldn't you like me to show you some spots?"

"Bug off, Buster. Before I tell your boss."

"I am the boss."

"That is beyond belief."

SHE didn't mind. She was in a burrowing frame of mind. This cozy haven: two rooms and a kitchen on the second story of a cut-up old town house. The floors creaked and were hilly. The "feature" was a real fireplace with stained-oak paneling and three carved cherubs supporting the mantel. They looked to her like Henry Kissinger in various stages of getting sloshed. She had named them Henry Winkum, Henry Blinkum, and Henry Nod.

She had fallen for the place the moment the real-estate lady opened the door the previous Wednesday. The light in the main room had been a clear swimmable liquid—zip, she was snorkeling off Cinnamon Bay on St. Thomas during that crackbrain trip with Greg, winter before last. When she had got a little bit preggers. The fertilization of the need for change. Moving into the room, she made vague breast-stroke motions and said to the real-estate lady, "This is it." The real-estate lady's face was thin; her neck, tendinous; fat didn't set in until somewhere below the fallen bosom. She was all tumbled down into rumphood. At the very moment when Elaine began to float in that buoyant light, the woman droned on about going to a class in something she called slimnastics. Every day, she said. The exercises only made her ravenous.

Number One Change in the new life in the new setting: Elaine Quinlan would attract no more confessional crap from hopeless people. Such talk was pollution in the clear air of possibility. In the old life her eyes had been too "feminine." No more. She would plate her eyeballs with chrome.

W̲HAT would rebirth be like? Her self had been in labor for so very long. Would she come into the world for the second time headfirst? Would she have to be held up by the heels and spanked, so she could start bawling "Me! It's me!" Would there be trauma? Only she would have changed; the world would not have been made good. Standing bewildered in the midden of her possessions dumped randomly around her by these two indifferent goons, she was not nearly so sure as she had been last Wednesday that these premises would cast a spell of magic over her. If she was enchanted, it was by the law of inertia. She thought of the job Greg had had two summers before, pacing jerkily back and forth in front of a movie theater dressed up as a mechanical toy, with a huge wind-up key sticking out of his back, moving his lips with metallic precision in sync with a recorded teaser for that week's show being barfed from a loudspeaker in his stovepipe hat. Back and forth, back and forth, with joints on toggle pins. She watched him sometimes, amazed by the metronomic inevitability of his actions. He said he used to become hypnotized by the repetitive movements and became convinced that he *was* wound up, that he worked on a coil spring. Oh, *damn* his eyes.

The black man lowered to the living room floor her open box of kitchen utensils with the C. S. Bell Model 2 (2MC) hand grain grinder visible on top. Having set the box down, he looked at the gadget and slowly shook his head. She felt embarrassed. She hadn't used the stupid thing for three years. Why had she kept it?

She asked if he'd mind putting that box in the kitchen.

He looked at her and, again, slowly shook his head. Meaning, apparently, yes, he did mind. But he moved the box.

A huge head—there was a small pudding of a face in the middle of it—leaned away from the jamb.

"Moving in?"

As if by reflex, Elaine stepped toward the door, full of the need to block the path of anyone capable of a gloppy opener like that one. A whole body was now framed there: of a compact little lady in a mauve velvet bathrobe and fuzzy green slippers, her head grossly swollen by a mass of curlers bunched under a pink paisley scarf she was wearing, tied at the nape. The colors!

"Where have you come from, dearie?"

Elaine ignored the question and snappishly said, "Mind stepping back and letting the animals through?"

With an "Oops, par' me," the lady stepped *forward*, right by Elaine, well into the room, and Elliott Gould loomed past with a sharp sound of inhaling.

"Always wanted to see the second-floor-back," the lady said, her fast black eyes shrewdly appraising Elaine's belongings, then lightly dusting baseboards and windowsills. Her eyebrows did a brief waltz when her glance landed on the three Henrys. "We had such an offish genmun living in here before. A quick slammer. He kept a real fast door, I'm telling you. They said he worked at Kelly and Newhouse. The morticians? I'm so glad *you've* come. Seriously, honey"—she was very sweet, she wasn't going to be satisfied with wiseass answers—"where'd you come from? I see the van has Ohio, Pennsy, and Jersey licenses."

Oh, *God*.

At once Elaine wondered whether she had said it out loud. Her hopes for pause, for a sealed place, for modulation, were crashing around her.

The black man was saying, "Where does this, uhn this . . . this . . ." He couldn't bring himself to give a name to her Kovacs lamp: milk-glass globe on an overarching chrome arm.

"In the bedroom. . . . I've come from Beantown."

The lady lowered her eyelids discreetly in the face of such an obvious lie. Then she looked straight at Elaine and said, "Look, honey, I'm getting in your hair. I'm Mary Calovatto. I live in the front. I . . . I picked a poor time . . ."

"No no no. Be my guest. No. Truthfully. I've come from Philly."

"You can't tell what to believe these days," the lady said, a bit too openly pleased that Elaine's guard had dropped for a moment. "What brought you to New Haven?"

"I couldn't really tell you."

"What work do you do?"

"Christ, Mrs. uh—"

"Calovatto."

"Calovatto." Elaine could find nothing more to say.

The swarthy lips were pressed somewhat tightly together, forming little ciliated pleats of hurt. "I just— They don't have a Welcome Wagon around here. I thought you'd—. There are things you should know."

Elaine, feeling brutish, did her best to look receptive.

Mrs. Calovatto checked to make sure the movers were both out of earshot. "The janitor. You have to get your lock changed. The janitor—you can't imagine him. The thing is, he has a master key. It's routine they give him a master key."

"Thank you. And now—"

"Oh, honey, don't take it so hard. We all have to make a move once in a while."

The next thing Elaine knew, she was in the arms of this Mrs. Calovatto, picking up powerful whiffs of garlic as she caught her breath between sobs.

"I just drove off," she told Mary Calovatto over coffee in the Calovattos' kitchen. On the wall facing Elaine there was a blue-toned litho of Jesus in a long nightgown, holding a shepherd's crook. "I didn't even tell him I was leaving. I took his MG—it was his *father's* MG—and went to the bank and drew out five hundred dollars, and then I took off. I didn't have a clue what I was going to do. Oooh, I felt bad. The top was all torn, so it had to be down. My hair was whipping around. When I got to the Lincoln Tunnel, they stopped me at the toll booth. All these photographers started taking pictures of me. Flash bulbs. Microphones. Like I was a pop star. They said I was the ten millionth car to go through the tunnel. A reporter asked me where I was going. I said, 'I don't know. I don't *know*,' and burst into tears. I looked in the papers the next day, I bought early and late editions, but I never found the story. I didn't guess the *Times* would carry it, but I thought for sure it would be in the *Daily News* and the *Post*."

"What did you do with the car?"

"Oh, shit, he activated his parents' lawyers. Don't worry, he got his heap back."

"But you got your things, too," Mrs. Calovatto said with

some satisfaction, dipping her mound of curlers toward the apartment next door.

"You bet your butt I did. And some of his, too."

"What made you pick New Haven?"

"God knows. Clean slate. I have a couple pretty good friends here."

"Yale?" Mrs. Calovatto looked as if she did not really want an answer to that question.

"Sort of. One of them's a researcher for a linguistics prof. One of them's a graduate student. They're not *that* good friends. I don't have any really good friends." Elaine tricked out a wan smile. "Except you."

For a second Mrs. Calovatto looked as if she might faint.

For two days Elaine puttered around the apartment and went out for walks, to get the lay of the neighborhood. She had had no idea, rooting and tooting here and there with the real-estate lady, that she had landed in such a fine part of town. She walked round and round the wooded square; sycamores and oaks and maples and a few surviving elms were putting out their first yellow-green fists over a statue of Christopher Columbus, who held a globe in one hand and a navigator's dividers in the other, and who was surprisingly thin; for some reason she had always pictured Columbus as a great tubful of pasta. The houses on the square were gems. Her eyes lighted on a concave mansard roof with patterned slate between its dormers and with an iron-work balustrade hemming in the aerials. A lazy dozing giant of yearning turned over in Elaine when she thought of the craftsmanship that had gone into that roof; she had used to lean over her drawing board, confident of her spatial taste, dreaming up dymaxion love nests, pyramids of expanded perception, environments open to universal loops. All those visions were slack in her now. She hated her half-heartedness. But a spirit of mischief perked up in her as she saw clues to envy and vanity in these houses with proud historic-district plaques by their front doors: one portico with modest Doric columns, the next with stately Ionian, a third with triumphant, down-putting Corinthian. What total culture! Besides all that Greek Revival, she ticked off an English Regency canopy porch, Art Deco windows, Queen Anne embroidered brickwork, a Norman turret, a New Orleans cast-iron balcony, and an Italian Renaissance church with a little dome like a glans at the top of its tower. Across the square from her apartment was a wing of a modern school building, designed with tact so that its low façade along the square carried out the motif of adjoining classical porches. She walked through the school grounds. There were ringing sounds of recess. Girls shrieked under a basketball hoop. Groups of boys conspired in satiny windbreakers with cursive hot-colored letters on the backs: Warheads, Shafters, Zuks. Attached to the school was a senior citizens' center. Some elderly men, speaking thick Napoletano, were playing bocce on a court. She walked beyond into a zone of cobwebs and mildew. Houses wore tarpaper shingles. Autos parked on the street had American flags on their aerials; a stripped-down carcass of a car squatted in a rubbled lot. Men were gathered on a double-house stoop, laughing loud, in sleeveless undershirts, their tattoos exposed. Worn-out women were on another porch, inclining their heads to each other, whispering. A dog barked in every dooryard.

MARY Calovatto told Elaine that her husband Giulio worked for Southern New England Telephone as a road man, and she said he could call a pal in the office and get Elaine a phone pronto. Elaine said she got a feeling of tightness in her throat when she talked on the phone, and once, when a man told her how, on transatlantic calls, each person's voice is broken into tiny bits and scrambled with hundreds of other voices and jammed overseas, and then is unscrambled and reassembled into intelligent speech with personality in it, she started coughing and almost choked—just hearing that. Now they were talking about sending voices as light impulses through glass wires. Elaine said resonance mattered to her; distance in space mattered to her; looks in the eye mattered to her.

Mary Calovatto looked puzzled. "Never mind, honey," she said, patting Elaine's hand. "Giulio'll put some goose grease in there. You'll get your phone."

A ND she did, the next day.

Deciding she had to start somewhere, she called Ruth Greenhelge, the one who worked for the linguistics professor.

"Come see me," she said, with the tight feeling in her throat. "I have this dream apartment."

"I wouldn't call that a dream neighborhood."

"It's heaven. What are you talking about?"

"Wooster Square? You've got Eyeties. You've got Jigaboos. You've got Polacks. You've got Litvaks. Conte School used to be one hundred percent nice respectable Italians, now it's half Jigs."

"Come *on*, Ruth."

"Wait and see. A mugging every night."

S HE called her mother.

"Hello, Mom."

"Lainie? Why haven't you called?"

"I *am* calling, Mom."

"Six weeks. Not a word."

"I've got some news you'll like."

"You never had any consideration for your mother."

"Mom. Listen."

"From the time you were a baby."

"I'm not living with Greg any more."

"You could call me collect. I've always said that. *What?*"

"I've left the bastard."

"Child. Child. Your tongue." Then: "Oh, Lainie, I'm so glad. He never was right for you. I knew that from the beginning."

"You might have told *me* that."

"Would you have listened?"

"No. My God, no. What a fucking nerve, deciding who's *right* and who's *not right!*"

"Lainie! I should wash your mouth out with soap and water."

A KNOCK.

Elaine went to the door and found there a man with Swiss-chocolate skin, about forty, she judged, dressed in old Army fatigues, with a misshapen jaw and a down look.

"I'm the 'stodian, ma'am."

"Oh, good. I'm Elaine Quinlan."

"Yes'm. I seen the mailbox. How long you fixing to stay?"

"I don't know—what's your name?"

"Justy."

"I don't know how long. It depends."

"Got to collect for the garbage disposable, Missus Quillan. Two dollar a week."

"For the what?"

"Trash, ma'am."

"How come? You mean the city charges to take it away?"

"No'm. It's a regulation."

"Whose regulation?"

"Don't ask me, ma'am. Just a regulation."

"Does everyone have to pay?"

"Oh, yes'm."

"Listen, while you're here, I have a problem in the kitchen. Come in, Justy."

She turned, and the janitor followed her. She heard a clicking sound as he walked. She looked back and saw that he had an artificial left leg.

"What happened to you?"

"Nam, ma'am."

"Oh, God, I'm sorry."

"You go tell that to the Vet'ans 'Ministration, ma'am. They got my jawbone, too." He pushed his chin to the right with his left hand, for her to see the ruins.

The refrigerator door would not swing shut of its own weight. With much clanking of the plastic limb Justy kneeled and turned the right front foot-screw up, until the door clunked to; then he evened out the other supports. Elaine gave him the two dollars, and he left, *clickety-clickety*.

M ARY Calovatto gave shopping advice, gratis. Right around the corner on Wooster Street were a couple of pizza palaces, the real thing. The most convenient market was just beyond them—a neighborhood place, Cavaliere's. Mrs. Calovatto was everything Elaine dreaded becoming but could not help liking. Her sorrow was that she was childless. It seemed that Giulio could not forgive her for her barrenness. Elaine pointed out that he might have been sterile. "I know," Mrs. Calovatto said, "but he given up on me." When Elaine told her that she had had an abortion, so much blood drained out of Mrs. Calovatto's face that she looked as if she had been zapped by fate and was turning into an albino. But very soon there was a new rush of rosiness—Mrs. Calovatto obviously had quick springs of inquiry in her—and Elaine saw glints in her eyes, jagged bits of brown glass, flashes, it seemed, of curiosity, envy, and even speculation on her own account.

"By the way," Elaine said, "do you pay two bucks a week to have the garbage taken away?"

"Did that son of a gun pull that one on you? Watch out, honey. That man is a common criminal."

"I felt sorry for him."

"Don't be a softy. You watch it, now. Those people are in-filtrating this entire area."

Chapter 2

THIS woman leans hipslung against the wall not far from the door. It is not possible to tell whether she is married—there is only a last name, Brainard, on the card in the slot by the doorbell—but it seems that she is a bit bleary and gone. Her face is flushed, there seems to be some kind of tropical fever in her eyes, whose whites mock their name, as she watches the young man work.

He is bent over putting the finishing touches on a deadbolt rim lock.

His long hair is pulled back in a ponytail. He is wearing a clean coverall of blue twill with *Safe-T Securit-E Syst-M* embroidered in gold on the back. *Eddie* is written in the same gold like a pledge over his heart.

She has exclaimed at his workmanship. The chisel cuts he has made in the jamb and trim to accommodate the loop plate of the lock are as if machine-squared. To begin with, his sharpening of the chisel was like foreplay; the foot-long whetstone—one big erogenous zone. His eyes are soapy. He is *beautiful*. She shifts hips.

These two have had much satisfactory conversation. He has told her he had a brief stay at Reed College. The only subject he liked was chemistry. "I built up a whole philosophy of life in terms of interactions and energy levels." She has informed him that her breasts are full of silicone. This has been the occasion for elaborate compliments. He has a sunny disposition. There is a lot going on in his head. She shifts hips again. The fit of the loop plate into the chisel cuts is incredibly snug. He has very strong feelings about beer cans littering up National Parks.

He is done and she looks sad. He closes the door and turns the lock button on the inside. The lock clicks smartly shut. Then he goes outside and closes the door again and works the lock several times with the key.

He opens and enters. "You understand you have to lock the door with the key every time you go out, and you want to lock it from the inside when you come in. This doesn't work by itself like a latch lock."

She nods. She looks woebegone.

Then he glances at the chips on the floor and asks, "Where's your vacuum cleaner?"

"Oh, don't bother," she says.

"I don't leave till I've cleaned up," he says.

"Then come in and have a cup of coffee," she says, brightening.

She might have suggested beer if he hadn't been so fierce about the parks. He said earlier he had seen most of them in a microbus he used to own. It had scenes painted on it combining dinosaurs and Unidentified Flying Objects, delicately airbrushed in Day-Glo and porch-and-trim enamel. That, he has said, was "in a younger period." He declines the coffee. He has to get to another job, he says.

"About that vacuum cleaner," he says.

Sudden sunshine. "Come with me," she says. Up to this time he has stayed right by the door. This is her first opportunity to draw him into her web. "Let's see," she says. "I was house cleaning before you came. I think I left it in here." She leads him into the bedroom. The silicone upholstery is prominent. The bed is unmade. There is an awkward pause, caused by the absence of the vacuum. His look remains high-voltage and hard-assed. She wilts a little and leads him to the kitchen, where the vacuum is hiding in the broom closet.

MACABOY breezes out of the half-timbered apartment house at 402 Whitney Avenue with twenty smackeroos in his pocket. Eight for the lock, twelve for labor. Here is something quite surprising: The company for which he works, Safe-T Securit-E Syst-M, does not have a truck. Chained to a lamppost on the sidewalk is a bicycle which has an undersized front wheel, so as to accommodate, forward of the handlebars, an unusually large metal basket. Into this basket he lowers his wooden tool box. He twirls the knob of a combination lock and undoes a chain heavy enough to anchor an aircraft carrier. He drapes this crosswise over both shoulders, becoming for a moment, in his struggle with the chain, one of the sons in the Laocoön. Then he wheels the bike off the curb and takes off. The handlebars are high, rising away from the steering post in a capital V. He sits up like a Canadian Mountie. He fiddles with the speed shift lever. He steadily churns his knees. Going down Whitney he whistles an aria from *Aïda*. *O terra addio; addio, vale di pianti.* Radames and Aïda are sealed in the great stone tomb, this is their *Liebestod*. Macaboy whistles it merrily. At the Berzelius triangle he takes the left fork, breasting the oncoming one-way traffic. In the first block of Church Street he dismounts and chains his bike to a lamppost. He lifts his tool box out and carries it into the building with him.

IN the outer office of Helena Beadle Real Estate sits Liz Roecake, Mount Holyoke '71, wasting her education at a gunmetal desk. The office is a blizzard of brochures. Liz wears braids. Macaboy rests his tool box on the floor in front of the desk.

"Hello, sweet potato."

"Eduardo!"

Just above a whisper: "The dragon in?"

"No. She's out showing the Coliseum to a family of midgets."

"What else is new?"

"Hey, a woman named Brainard just called."

"She's the one I was just at. Something wrong?"

"Said she was *most* impressed with your what she called artisanship. So *reasonable*, too! She wanted to thank Helena Beadle Real Estate for recommending you. What did you do for her, Eddie?"

"It's a hard life." He is grinning.

"Truly, she was breathless."

"She has knockers the size of soccer balls."

"*Chacun à sa* . . . Listen, bad one, *Oh! Calcutta!*'s at the York Square. Want to catch?"

"Can't tonight. Got any new suckers?"

Liz passes off his refusal without a flicker. "Wait a minute," she says. "Yeah. There was one the other day. Wooster Square area. Madam says she was a toothsome little biddy. Lost soul type. Maybe she'd be impressed with your artisanship, Fast Eddie."

"Come on, Liz. This is bread."

"Yeah, like pump-her-nick?" She shuffles some papers. "Let's see here." She finds a file card. "Elaine Quinlan. Thirty-two Academy Street. It would be a new phone, if any."

He writes in a notebook, says to Liz, "You're a living doll."

"Living?"

H E tools up Chapel, whistling. Banks right, onto Park. A couple of faggots are already out, in broad daylight, at the popular pickup corner, Park and Edgewood. Macaboy has passed these two youths here before, his heart has sunk as he watched them—for he can see the corner from the back window of his digs—getting into strange cars; they now wave to him as he swoops left into Edgewood. "Ah so!" Macaboy calls out to them with the bold, guttural, grunting voice of a Samurai. "Rots of ruck!"

Macaboy lives on the ground floor of one of the toy houses on Lynwood Place, famous in the past for having been broken into once a week. He has converted it into a fortlet. He leans his bike beside the door and takes from his tool box the leather case containing his sixteen sets of picks. He selects a delicate forked pressure wrench and a medium rake and goes to work on his own deadbolt lock, just to keep his hands tuned. It takes patience. He has installed a Farleigh-Munson Eversure, hard as a Brazil nut to crack. He hates the private-eye shows on the tube—Cannon sticks a gizmo in a keyhole, one diddle and he's in. Picking a decent lock is not like that. It's breathholding work, he tells people. Requires a lover's fingertips. If you're patient you can just barely feel the pin tumblers tick into lodgment, like the barest flutterings of the wings of a dying Polyphemus. Day after day pedestrians stroll past, and they see Macaboy bent over, obviously picking a lock, and what do they do? They walk on. They must be spaced out on too many of those mystery shows, they assume he's a plainclothes good guy making sure that crime will pay only so long as it entertains. Or else they have a load in their pants and don't want anyone to know. This time it takes him about eight minutes until *click*, he opens the door. He wheels his bike inside.

Tʜɪs apartment is one large room with a kitchenette you could play sardines in, a bathroom just big enough for two to take a shower together; but the generous main room has three zones, each so distinctive as to seem a separated space.

Against the south wall is a locksmith shop: a long bench

with several key machines, for cylindrical, pin-tumbler, and flat keys; two vises; and hammers, files, chisels, picks, drills, wrenches, screwdrivers, all hung in their proper places on wallboard hooks. Half the wall, to the right of the window, is given over to rows and rows of key blanks of most of the famous makes, on hooks, labeled, showing the symmetries of diligent inventory.

Along the east wall is a carpentry shop: another immaculate bench, another array of tools hung on wallboard hooks in fussy order. Not a grain of sawdust in sight. Everything oiled and sharpened and dusted.

In the angle between the north and west walls are a young man's living quarters—a catastrophe of failed training. Clothes kicked off onto the floor, sneakers and hiking boots and Earth Shoes estranged from mates, bedclothes giving hints of epic past contests of flesh or dream, records in a heap on the floor, dusty stereo speakers, dirty dishes in the sink, damp towels on the bathroom floor, signs of haste, signs of torpor, broken cups and resolutions—signs, Macaboy sometimes thinks, of the wreckage of his psyche. Or else, seen in a single panning shot along with the two obsessively tidy shops, signs of a wacky sense of relative importances in a not yet firmed organism.

He puts three platters of Nathan Milstein's recording of the Bach partitas and sonatas on his record player and turns on the machine.

He unzips and removes his company coverall, works on an oil spot on the left leg with Carbona, puts the coverall on a coat hanger, and hangs it in the closet. *This* he takes care of.

A long shower. He smoothes out the water on his skin with one of the damp towels. He walks around in the buff for a while to dry off, takes the Bach off and puts The Who on, then rummages in his wardrobe on the floor and comes up with some jeans and a tee shirt, which he puts on.

At his lockeyist's bench, getting bitting numbers and root depths from a Kanjan code book, he makes cuts in a pair of blank keys of that brand for a knob lock he plans to install the next morning.

After that, with Joni Mitchell on, he scarfs some Moroccan sardines out of a can, with Kirin beer and Arab bread; then he brews some lapsang souchong.

He reads *Nostromo* for a couple of hours.

By now it is nine o'clock—the best time. He picks the phone up off the floor near the head of the bed, and he lies on his side on the bed and dials Information.

"Hello."

"Is this Mzz Elaine Quinlan?"

"Yes?"

"I'm calling for Safe-T Securit-E Syst-M, Incorporated. The company has asked me to put a few questions to you about the security of your apartment."

"I . . . I don't know exactly what you mean. You mean a guard? There's a janitor that works around the building."

"No no, Mzz Quinlan, I mean your personal apartment. It's a question of a person living alone in an apartment."

Silence.

"Especially in an old building. I presume there's a buzzer latch on the main door? Those buzzer locks are worthless. There's always one tenant in every building who'll trip the latch when *any*body rings, no matter who it is."

"May I ask what you're selling?"

"Safety, Mzz Quinlan. My company argues for sound locks, as opposed to alarm systems. But if you choose alarms, we have 'em. You name it, we have 'em. Magnetic, ultrasonic, microwave, light-source—we have 'em. But we prefer sturdy locks. We have a slogan: 'A premium lock beats an insurance premium.' "

He has kept his voice upbeat, very courteous, but the woman's voice says, "This is *disgusting*, to try to make a sale by playing on fears."

"It's a real world, baby. You know, you have these shit-kickers running around."

Silence.

"The janitor you were talking about, bet he calls himself a custodian."

"What does that prove?"

"Nothing, nothing. How old is the building you're in?"

Silence.

"Thirty-two Academy Street? I can practically tell you. Our company knows this city inside out. Wooster Square was laid out in 1825. Most of the houses were built within the next fifteen years. So let's say a hundred and twenty-five years. Of course, everything rides on when the latest renovations were made. I'm thinking of doors. Our company places great stress on doors. We're not just locksmiths. We make doors, Mzz Quinlan."

Silence.

"You may be all right, doorwise. These new buildings, you see, these cheapjack builders face the doorjamb with a one-by-five board, wet pine, practically as soft as balsa wood, and anybody could come along and tie a piece of toweling around his shoe, to muffle it, and he could boot the door, and if he held onto the knob as he did it, hell, he could tear the whole strike plate and everything out of there, and you'd never hear it, if you were in bed and asleep."

Silence, then finally the woman's voice: "You make me want to puke. I *hate* cerebral palsy victims that somebody makes phone you and sell you guaranteed five-year electric light bulbs and you buy them because you're well and they burn out two hours after you put them in."

Silence, then the man: "Still listening?"

Silence.

"All my company wants is for you to feel safe."

"I *felt* safe till you called. You're worse than a breather. If I could trace this call . . ."

"Mzz Quinlan—"

"How'd you get my name?"

"If you decide to do something about your lock—or your door—don't go to just any locksmith. A lot of people are going into locksmithing these days. The company knows of a man, a former operative of our own, matter of fact, now runs a locksmithing school on the west coast, he teaches it in a high school, and he tells the kids who sign up for the course, you've got to get yourself registered and fingerprinted. Fully half of 'em don't show up the next day. You can guess why. Here in this state there's no regulation of locksmiths whatsoever. Are you listening? They have these locksmithing correspondence courses. There's many a prison inmate taking those courses right today."

"Disgusting disgusting disgusting."

"Remember the name. Safe-T Securit-E Syst-M. First word is S-a-f-e-hyphen-capital-T. We're in the book."

"Go fuck yourself."

He hangs up and lies back on the rumpled bedclothes with his hands folded behind his head. His face is as readable as the large-type edition of *The New York Times*. Behind it, were there a mind reader present, could be seen the myriad jumble of that busy head, but with one thought riding boatlike on the brain waves: *That was some voice.*

Chapter 3

Mrs. Calovatto took to inviting Elaine for coffee every morning about eleven. Her espresso would have lifted a Boeing 747 off the ground. She said, "Walk up to Malley's with me, honey. It's only seven, eight blocks. You got to see the important stores."

"O.K."

Elaine was waiting for the famous metamorphosis to happen to her. She wished to God she had never seen lugubrious Henry in those dopey cupids. She had been pushing and pulling her flotsam around for days, like Little Toot, the brave tug. Or what was the name of that undersized railroad engine in the other story?—*I-think-I-can, I-think-I-can* . . . She was beginning to feel as if she inhabited baby books. She lived a life of goo goo and bibble bibble. Lifting an ashtray involved a tremendous struggle for small-motor mastery. Yet she had certainly not been reborn. She disliked what she had been, and was. She felt increasing revulsion at all the clutter she had piled up in the past couple of years; she thought she and Greg must have fallen for every trendy item that came along. Candles with scents of the casbah, classy underground sheets like the London *Oz*, roach clips with semiprecious stones, fiberglass statuary, banana incense sticks, vegetarian toothpaste, shoes with boat-shaped platforms on which you could pitch and roll as if at sea, a book printed on edible paper so if you really dug it you could make it part of yourself—fads that mocked the bourgeoisie but took some good solid cash to buy. Could she really blame any of that shit on Greg? Hadn't she really been the mad shopper? . . .

And besides, that spook on the phone the other night. She had slept badly ever since. Yes, she'd like to get out on the streets.

Mrs. Calovatto reached back to undo her scarf. Unveiling of a sculpture. Elaine had never once seen Mary Calovatto out of her curlers. The arms, now languidly up, like a Matisse odalisque's, were soft-round, pale-skinned, with black hairs on the forearms; the hands had short fingers with flat ends, their skin was from the Avon Lady, the bone structure was fragile, the motions were slightly awkward like those of the spoor-hunting flippers of an adolescent. The knot yielded, and Mary Calovatto lifted away scarf, curlers and all. The curlers were not engaged with her hair at all; they were sewn to the scarf in rows, and they came right away from her head.

"Jesus," Elaine said. "Excuse me, but—"

"Haven't you ever seen a set of these?" Mrs. Calovatto held up the scarf by two corners, curlers facing Elaine. "It just makes you feel so good to wear them—makes you feel like you're getting ready to go out on a date. Know what I mean?"

She combed out her perm—every curl a whelky spiral, no need of plastic help—and they left.

Outdoors, Mary Calovatto put her short legs to work. Elaine's sandals flapped on the sidewalk, and she grew breathless; she was in gruesome condition. She thought the two of them must make a picture. The wax-skinned dark lady with permed black hair, in an imitation pongee dress over a mighty fortress of a foundation, the skirt shielding the shame of knees—yet high heels like castanets tapping out invitations; and the other woman, trying to keep up with her companion at a shuffling half run, with long straight brown hair, wearing jeans a bit white-threaded around the ass, and bouncy there, and in a maroon velour pullover, braless. The beauty part of the picture must have been that these two were talking and laughing and having a really fine time together, as if they were peas in a pod.

At the big store Mary Calovatto led the way to the sports department, where she ran those floppy, virginal hands over some seventy pairs of men's swimming trunks. She chose two, both full in the seat and long in the shank—a wild red plaid and a Hawaiian print: pineapples, surfers, hula girls.

"Oh, good," she said to the bald salesman behind the counter, a plump pycnic type who was dressed as if for a noon wedding in a dark suit, a striped shirt, a white collar, and a solid silver-gray tie. "You look *just* the right size. I never can tell Giulio's size except by a person. Come out here," she said, dribbling her fingers around the end of the counter and into the open in front of herself.

The clerk came warily out from his sanctuary. "Very *good*," Mrs. Calovatto said. "Just *right*. Turn around."

He faced away from her. Like a good soldier during an inspection, he was sucking in his gut, which now, however, seemed to be coming out behind under an assumed name. By way of measurement, she ran her hand flutteringly right down to the bottom of this protuberance, causing the clerk to execute an astonished bump, followed by a tiny involuntary grind.

"You're him to a square inch," she said. "I could have married *you*. Try them on." She reached the trunks out for him to take.

He held one pair in fingertips at his hips.

"No no no no no," she said. "You'll have to try them on."
Seeing him hesitate, she said sharply, "You have dressing
rooms, don't you?"

He shot away with a bunny hop, looking this way and
that.

"Isn't it kind of rushing the season, swimming?" Elaine
asked.

"We're going away a week from Monday. Giulio's vacation. Imagine us, the Virgin Islands!"

Elaine felt suddenly cold in the hands and feet. "How
long?"

"Aren't you cute, honey! You look real shocked."

"I got this creepy phone call the other night."

THE Calovattos were going to be away for three weeks.
Giulio got two weeks' regular vacation, and he had accumu-
lated an extra week in overtime. Elaine was more surprised by
the intensity of her reaction than she was by the reaction itself. She told Mrs. Calovatto about the call—how grossed out
she had been by that scare merchant. Mrs. Calovatto didn't
seem to think anything of it.

"What I can't understand is why I stayed on the phone so
long."

"Maybe he was making sense, honey."

"It was so crass."

Mrs. Calovatto said that was nonsense, Elaine should have
taken advantage of the nice young man, and she reminded
Elaine of what she had said about the need for a new lock
because of the janitor's having a master key. Then she said,
"Look, honey, before I go I'll take you down to meet the
Plentaggers. They live in first-floor-back. He's in pesticides.
They're homey people. They'll watch out for you."

Elaine thought she must have looked as if she would fly
into Mrs. Calovatto's arms again, because Mrs. Calovatto

hastily said, "See here, dearie, we're not going to the end of the world. It's only three weeks."

The salesman came away from the dressing rooms, once again looking all around. After a manner of speaking the swimsuit—the Hawaiian number—fitted him. Besides the trunks he was wearing black shoes and black ankle-length socks with silver clocks.

"Oh, dear," Mrs. Calovatto said. "You need sun."

Chapter 4

Every morning, long before the undergraduate metabolism stirs to the new day's moiling, a dignified gentleman in a gray sharkskin suit and a pork-pie hat, with a large attaché case and a shopping bag from The Pottery Bazaar, ranges along the sidewalk of Park Street discreetly ransacking the trash barrels outside Davenport and Pierson Colleges. Macaboy, out early himself on this Tuesday in dogwood time, sees him and feels that the indicators of the Macaboy horoscope must be in harmonious equipoise. It is good luck to meet this courtly fisherman in the seas of American waste. Macaboy has chatted with Mr. Tilton in the past—between barrels. Macaboy has enough savoir-faire to have grasped that you do not surprise a man of Mr. Tilton's class at the lip of a garbage can. You may talk to him, gent to gent, in the pauses of the quest. But whenever Macaboy sees from a distance that the hand digging in the drifts of built-in obsolescence has come upon a *thing* of mysterious virtue, which then rises up like a most-desired gift from a Christmas stocking—an out-of-date copy of *Oui*, a burned-out Norelco electric razor, an empty Old Grand-Dad bottle, the endoskeleton of a McIntosh amplifier, a left Adidas sneaker (the right, out at toe, has been dropped back)—the expression on Mr. Tilton's face infuses a wonderful radiance into Macaboy's constantly flagging hopes for joys in this miserable earthly coil and for decent competence in harp-playing beyond it. The month of May brings a bumper harvest: the seniors of the college are jettisoning their youth. Now when he leaves a cluster of barrels Mr. Tilton's pace bounces up and down as does the Dow-Jones index; he rises and dips like a flying swan on the heels and balls of his feet.

"Good morning, Mr. Tilton!"

"Good morning, Mr. Attaboy!" Mr. Tilton *knows* the real name; this is his speed at seven thirty in the morning.

"Beautiful day."

"Not really," Mr. Tilton says, as if he were telling the best news in weeks. "Did you hear the pollution counts this morning? Carbon monoxide is forty-one milligrams. Sulfur dioxide: four-twenty micrograms. Particular matter: two-ninety. Photochemical oxidants: two-ten. The Turnpike is Murder, Incorporated. There's a heat inversion."

Mr. Tilton's eyes rise to heaven, where the programmer of this meteorological accident is presumed to have His console.

Macaboy fakes a deep, deep cough.

Mr. Tilton, his gaze level again, smiles a knowing smile, and nods.

M ACABOY felt exalted even before he met Mr. Tilton: he is headed out to Branford to buy lumber. Good wood makes him nigh unto horny. He appreciates the look of the grain of well-cured hardwood from near the heart of the bole almost as much as he admires the sight of the circle of tiny goose-fleshlike bumps in the corona around an erected nipple. Yesterday, in the course of flinging a telephonic net across Fairfield and New Haven counties, he learned that Medary's Builders Supply in Branford has a stack of two-inch walnut that has been sitting there *for eight years*. Who wants solid walnut when you can get it veneered onto pine plywood?

Macaboy wants it! Macaboy leches after it! He has borrowed the notorious Chevvy camper belonging to Finn Okvent, the second-year graduate student who takes computer science in the electrical engineering department and lives in the micro-flat above Macaboy's rooms. Thanks to the buoyant gas in this Okvent's skull, located in the pan of bone usually reserved for a brain, the man has a specific gravity just under that of air, and he floats around, about eight inches off the ground, dreaming up flow charts and loops of command and elegant algorithms. Using his camper as a laboratory, Okvent is in the process of inventing a minicomputerized fuel conservator for piston engines, and as a consequence, this death-machine of his, in the present state of its development, has an alarming way of alternately leaping out from under the accelerator, like a whippet goosed with English mustard by a corrupt dogtrack attendant, and abruptly stalling, usually in the middle lane of a freeway. But Okvent is generous and close at hand, and whenever Macaboy needs transport beyond the capacities of his bike, he borrows the killercar.

Mr. Tilton was right about the Turnpike. Okvent's stuttering camper moves like a Jacques Cousteau minisub through deeps of poison, and Macaboy can *feel* his bronchial infundibula turning black. He is, nevertheless, still miraculously alive at the Foxon reservoir. At the Branford toll. Even when he parks in the Medary lot, on Main Street, Branford.

AT the order desk stands a young man in khaki clothes holding a transistor radio to his ear, like a hot poultice on a sore place. He is in a trance of concentration. At eight twelve in the morning The Temptations are giving the lucky world "With These Hands."

Macaboy shouts, "I called yesterday about some walnut."
"Wha?" Annoyed.
"Walnut!"
"*Wha?*"

"Lumber! Walnut!"

"Plywood's over there." Thumb slantwise over the shoulder. "Pick out your own."

"No! Solid walnut!"

"Solid? We don't have none."

"I was told by telephone."

The young man, without removing the compress, mashes a button on a squawk box. "Squeegie, we got any walnut?"

A hollow voice comes out of the speaker. "On the racks, man."

"Nah plywood. He wants solid."

"Walnut? Come on, Cube, I ain't had my coffee yet."

Cube turns off the squawk box. "We ain' got none."

"Where's your boss?"

Now Cube lowers the radio and cuts the volume. Suddenly removed from the traffic jam of decibels, the young man's voice pierces like an ambulance siren. "Man, I ain' got all day."

Macaboy persists.

M R. Medary, a tiny, bred-out Yankee with a bulging bald head and a network of veins on his nose like a roadmap of the glacier-scraped domain of John Calvin, stands now at the order desk beside Cube, who is lost to "Everything's Going to Be All Right." Mr. Medary says it was he who fielded Macaboy's call yesterday. Yes, he knows exactly where the walnut is. It is, he says, in two-by-twelves and two-by-sixes, sixteen-footers. "What sizes do you wish?"

Macaboy says he'll need two cuts ten inches wide and twenty-six long. From the smaller stock he wants two cuts of six by eighty, six of four by twenty-six, and six of four by forty.

Mr. Medary, having waited eight years to unload this ill-bought consignment, is seen to experience a sharp letdown. Is that *all?*

Oh, Macaboy says, the company will be back for more, much more, later on.

Mr. Medary asks, "What is this for, anyway?"

"A door."

"A door? But we have ready-made doors. All you have to do is hang them."

"I know," Macaboy says, "but our company specializes in custom-built doors."

Mr. Medary shakes his head. "It'll take us a while to cut them up. Want the waste pieces? We'll have to charge you for them."

"Indeed I do," Macaboy says. "But if you wouldn't mind, I'd like to pick out the lengths and place the cuts."

Mr. Medary stretches his wild-turkey neck out to inspect Macaboy's ponytail, as if that might explain everything.

"Our company is exceedingly labor-intensive," Macaboy says, grinning.

Mr. Medary leads the way. The display room through which they walk rouses in Macaboy an abstracted rage. Oystershell plastic toilet seats, towel racks of metal about the same gauge as Reynolds Wrap, imitation ship's lanterns, stagecoach weather vanes, knotty-pine plywood with fake wormholes, aluminum screen doors with openwork hearts and porpoises. He wonders: Is the flow irreversible? No matter. He is soon outside in the metal-roofed lumber sheds where he can smell cured sap and believe that he feels the warmth of the decades of sunlight stored in the long fibers of tree trunks. And then his hand lies flat on a twelve-inch-wide plank of solid walnut. "Unreal!" he says.

Chapter 5

RUTH Greenhelge came to what was called dinner. From around the corner Elaine had fetched a pizza with peperoni and another with The Works. And some really bad real Chianti—they couldn't drink California grape because of Cesar Chavez's grape-pickers' strike.

After dinner they talked about Bennington days—Ruth had been a "pretty good" friend there—and at one point Elaine said, "Like a smoke? I stole a nickel of Colombian red of Greg's."

"God, Elaine, I'd be fired in a minute."

"Fired? You expecting Professor Ultra-Logic to bust in the door or something?"

Greenhelge, Elaine could see, had walked a hell of a mile since college. She'd been a mad-ass SDSer there, working up the daughters of corporation lawyers and shrinks and twelve-tone-scale composers to become fire-eating Fidelistas, Tupamaros, Venceremos, Congs, you name it in a foreign tongue. Crazies had come from all over New England to hear Greenhelge's speeches because she had fantastic legs. The radicals really dug the way the female hormones rippled in those incredible satin thighs quivering out of her working-woman's denim cutoffs; the Movement was totally man-dominated in those days. When Greenie hollered out short-order omelets of Herbert Marcuse and C. Wright Mills and Norman O. Brown she emphasized her most telling arguments with her pelvis, and the Ivy League workers of the world cheered to see the seat of social change bumping and grinding before their very eyes. No matter that her incisors were dangerous-looking—"wood-cutters," Greg had called them. From a middle distance Greenhelge could, as they say, start a riot. Now she was wearing pantyhose and talking straight *New York Times* Op-Ed page. The only subject she could sing the old tunes about was Yale policy on "affirmative action"— she cared about the hiring of women, not of minorities. She couldn't believe that Elaine had not yet found upwardly mobile employment.

"I guess I'm going to have to do *some*thing," Elaine said, to be agreeable. "I'm going kind of stir-crazy."

"I'm glad you've at least left Greg," Greenhelge said. "There was something—I can't put my finger on it exactly —something seedy about him."

At this judgment Elaine felt her first real pang of missing Greg. He could do such incredible imitations—Nixon and Chou En-lai toasting each other in the Great Hall of the Revolution in Peking, with an interpreter standing between them, taking all three parts in rapid flashes, with the most beautiful quick modulations of mouth and eyebrows, from Nixon's look-ma-I'm-changing-the-world smile, higher on the left side of the mouth than the right, to Chou's cool stare with a drawn-down upper lip, to the interpreter's expression of "I better get this right or my ass is chop suey." Somehow Greg could make Chou's eyebrows seem black and heavy, while Nixon's little ones looked as if the IRS would get them if he didn't backdate them.

Hooo, time to get off that stick. Change the sub. "Speaking of your prof coming through the door, I got this phone call a few nights ago," Elaine heard herself saying. "A locksmith. He wanted to come and hang a new door and install a burglar-proof lock. I almost took him up on it. He had such a sexy line. It was so sort of comforting, when you've moved to a strange city."

"Sounds like a pitchman. Watch out, honey bun."

"It was more than that. Greenie, remember how we used to talk about—." Elaine broke it off in midsentence. She had been about to say "openness," and she felt a sudden wrench —two violent contrary pulls, as if a parachute had just deployed over her to end a free fall. The downward pull toward sentimentality, fed by the memory of those sheltered days when choices were as easy to come by as balls of chewing gum in a penny vending machine; and the opposing force of sharp regret, of bitter loss, of clearer vision that saw nothing much good on the landscape. Where were the hopes of those days? Where the "openness"? Where, for that matter, the anger? Why, she suddenly wondered, was her account of the Safe-T Securit-E Syst-M phone call to Mrs. Calovatto so different from her version of it to Greenhelge? Was she trying to impress each of them in a different way? Didn't she have a mind of her own? She wished she could talk to Greg.

"Oh, shit, Greenie," she said. "What's made you so stuffy?"

ELAINE sat in her rocker with her album open on her knees. She leaned forward to look more closely at the picture of the dazzling couple: he was in an Esso pumpwinder's shirt, and she in a Mexican serape. Thus were lightly disguised a Dartmouth senior and a Bennington junior, leaning against a beat-up VW bug. God, she had a wigged-out way of baring her teeth whenever anyone flashed an Instamatic at her! As for Greg, he had crossed his eyes and puffed out his cheeks to show his full male beauty. Ha ha.

They met at the Ice Carnival. He was straight then. She began dating him. He organized art shows in Hopkins Center with an entrepreneurial flair, looked like a rampaging Visigoth on skis, trippingly spoke six languages, took long nightly

baths in loud music—the fallout of burnt calories around
him was as thick as the snow on Channel 7. Yet he was so
gentle with children!—had the three-year-old daughter of a
poli-sci prof on his shoulders half the time. He read all over
the place: Iris Murdoch, Turgenev, Ken Kesey, Hawthorne,
Isaac Asimov, Erich Fromm, Mark Twain. He had studied
letterpress printing with Ray Nash; he carried wizard designs in his eyeballs, but when it came to popping them out
on paper his intermediary fingers always got in the act, with
subtle, creative distortions that make things wobble. He did
a Krishnamurti poster, stunning in concept, that made you
feel, as you looked at it, as if a slight earthquake were taking
place. His hair was cut short in those days: he had been cam-
paigning for Senator McCarthy that fall, Clean for Gene. He
had small eyes, with an overhanging epicanthic fold that
made him look slightly, he said, gooky.

He was funny. Everything was a laugh. Everything that
should have been a warning was a ha-ha.

In freshman year he had borrowed his roommate's briar
pipe and had accidentally broken it while high. He was on
scholarship. His father worked in a paper mill in Saco. His
sister had fallen out of her tree on a bad acid trip at Bates,
ha ha ha, and the cuckoo's nest bills had cleaned the family
out; they hadn't started with much, certainly not with Major
Medical. Greg was chipping in. He hadn't a dime to spare. So
for a replacement for his friend's pipe he stole a meerschaum
at the Co-op and was caught. College probation, ha ha.

In sophomore year he and his roommate stripped their
dorm room—nothing left but four pillows on the floor, a
candle stand, an incense brazier, a vase with a single carnation in it most of the time: a décor that was like an electro-
magnet for campus cops who got off on narky games. Bust.
Pot and peyote in a duffel bag of Greg's in the bedroom, just
a nothing amount.

A double-breasted pinstripe lawyer whom the dean scraped
up bargained Greg a misdemeanor plea. (*Loud laughter.*)

In junior year he took his stand on Vietnam, turned in his draft card, was reclassified *1-A delinquent*, metamorphosed into a jellyfish, recanted, took his card back, and settled for a *3-S* deferment. That, she realized now and wished she had realized then, was the beginning of the end of Greg. At the time, it was all part of The Big Joke.

Between junior and senior years, Elaine and Greg went with a Slavic-studies group to Yugoslavia, Rumania, Russia. Greg loved quoting Pushkin and singing *"Ochi chorniye"* and crying with Russian kids they met. He told one bunch of natives on a street corner on Nevsky Prospekt in Leningrad that his group was from Mongolia and ate babies. He tried to enroll as an acting student at the Vakhtangov Theater in Moscow but was told he would have to spend a year with a lot of dusky third-worlders at Patrice Lumumba University getting sanitized, but he said, "I ain't up for living with furriners right now, it's the Russkies I like."

Elaine thought of him as Mr. Magic and had begun having intercourse with him just before the snapshot was taken beside the VW. That was why the expressions in the photo were so interesting. Her parents thought of them as "going steady" until about a year and a half later, when they got wind of the mechanical termination of her pregnancy. They were unable to put into clear language what they thought after that.

In the fall of his senior year Greg ran for president of the student body, but his printed campaign fliers were vague— spoke of universal love, of government ownership of the means of production of mary jane, and of his having seen the Living Theater once in Boston. His opponent, one Stanley Clapper, had a well-thought-out program for tearing down the university brick by brick. Greg wouldn't pat people on the back; he preferred going to the library and pulling down Mandelstam and reading reading reading. Clapper won going away, best laugh of all.

It was not so funny "living together" separately, in Hanover and Bennington, especially when Greg began expanding his consciousness chemically, and had a field of vision much taken up with whizzies, halos, and black holes. Elaine began to be aware of his flaw. He couldn't go all the way with anything. He wore costumes—the Andover student peeked out from under the Indian headband. He talked about moving off campus but never did. He extolled the Yippie revolution of style, but obscenities were like too-hot baked potato in his mouth. His caution could not save him. Even with drugs his conviction was tinged by affectation: he *talked* about people who shot up with crystal and came down with smack, and he kept a plastic marijuana plant in a clay pot in his room, and he called grass by what he said was its South African name, *dagga*.

It was even less good together in Boston later.

In Philly after that it was a horror show. It turned out that Mr. Magic produced rabbits out of a top hat with *a false crown*, and he really did saw Elaine in two.

She rocked in her rocker. She wanted so much from life. Her hair fell forward like a fringe around the album. The light grew dim on the couple leaning against the dented bug.

SHE woke up with a certainty that she had flown into a hawk's territory. She had heard *click click click click* nearby. In her living room? Her heart, hooked up to a compressor chisel, would have broken up concrete pavement. Her ears grew bigger and bigger, until they flapped in the dark like an elephant's ears. Still they could not hear breathing, or even plastic articulations. All they could hear were the heavy rigs shifting gears for the northbound speedup on I-91. In the morning she decided she must have dreamed the stealthy movements of a prosthetic limb.

Chapter 6

Mrs. Calovatto was as good as her word. After supper on Friday evening she took Elaine downstairs to meet the Plentaggers. Their apartment was a clearing hacked out of a rain forest. Everything was savannah green. Huge leaves spread themselves on all fabrics. Innumerable botanical prints made the vertical surfaces seem upended garden plots rather than walls. Elaine listened for Rima's bird-voice. The only thing that was missing from the living room was a sprinkler.

All this tropical greenery, sunstruck by a profusion of hundred-watt bulbs, made Mr. and Mrs. Plentagger look liverish, malarial. They were brimming at least with mental health, for they said yes sure they were up for taking Elaine under their wing a pleasure. Elaine felt a stab of panic. Mrs. Plentagger wrote their phone number on a lettuce-green memo pad and told Elaine not to hesitate to call.

"If we're out you'll get a recording," Mr. Plentagger told her. "It's sort of a commercial. Says"—and his voice dropped an octave—" 'This is your Supalgran man. Little plant pests hate me. If you hate them you'll love me. Please leave your name and number when you hear the signal.' " He looked receptive to applause.

"That's clever," Elaine said. "Isn't it?" she asked Mrs. Calovatto, really needing to know.

"Homer's such a card!" Mrs. Calovatto said.

Merle Plentagger broke into wild baritone laughter, apparently at the mere thought of some of her husband's witticisms. "He's poisonous!" she finally managed to croak.

Mrs. Calovatto joined in the guffawing. "He *sells* poison," she shouted to Elaine between waves of laughter.

Mr. Plentagger, looking gloomy, said, "Mary tells us you have terrariums. With terrariums you can keep pretty good control, though it's possible—I say possible—to have white fly, spider mite, mealybug. It's possible. Mildew. Mold . . ."

"You better let Homer look them over," Mrs. Calovatto said.

"My fittonia wilted," Elaine said. "But I think it was my fault. It didn't like me talking so much to my calathea." No one laughed at *her* little joke. She felt a need for a shift of ground. "Mary," she said, calling Mrs. Calovatto by her first name for the first time, "where are you staying on St. Thomas?"

"Place called Bluebeard's Castle."

"I know that place. In Charlotte Amalie. Groovy. But look, you *have* to go up to the outer end of the island to a place called Cinnamon Bay. For at least a day and a night. The sand is like talcum powder." Elaine had a sudden impulse which she could not fight down. "I got my ears fucked off on that sand. Remember the abortion I was telling you about? That they used the vacuum aspirator suction method for, like I was telling you? I bought the ticket to it on that sand. Don't miss it, Mary. Get Giulio out on that sand."

The pesticides man cleared his throat hard, as if it were all clogged up with aphids and cockchafers.

AFTERNOON rays poured in her living room window through a gauze of grime. She sat looking out on pretension and its obverse. She could see, off to the sun side, a cut through to Court Street, which had been, in her opinion, renewed till it hurt: the streetway was a mall, with planting up the middle in massive concrete boxes, and the façades of the houses were tricked out in bright colors, like the faces of clowns. Elaine had walked there and didn't like it. It was too rendered, too like a display of the latest office equipment or kitchen appliances. She much preferred the backyards she could now see on either side of the gap: rickety, cluttered, put out of mind—fine places for cats to howl and kids to pretend.

From time to time she got up to change a record; first she'd played some bluegrass, with banjos and whiny fiddles, and now she had on some high sweet gospel. Odd: she wasn't a country girl, her farming was all in glass jars; and she certainly wasn't churchy—the rebirth she awaited was not to be for Jesus. Of that, if of nothing else, she was sure. She remembered one of Greenhelge's speeches, from way back then. How rock was man's bag. Male supremacist energy, bang bang and not even thank-you-ma'am. All it had to say was that a good woman belonged under a man. Look at the stars, Greenie had shouted. Ever hear of boy groupies? Try to name some female instrumentalists. Two horns with Sly Stone, and two drummers, Ruth Underwood with Hamilton Face Band and Maureen Tucker with Velvet Underground. And what about the songs? Nothing but raging hard-ons, if you analyzed them: "Man and a Half," "Born to Be Wild," even "Do Right Woman." "What b.s.!" Greg had said after the meeting was over. "That chick's arbor grows sour grapes." The stuff he used to like to hear. Led Zeppelin. The Yardbirds. B. B. King. Steppenwolf. Joe Cocker. Jeff Beck. Frank Zappa. Jefferson Airplane. Elaine's taste had drifted away from thumping and smashing, toward more reflective sounds. She sat now by the window, pedaling her rocking chair, cantering through the universe. The yellow disk beyond the gauze didn't seem to be in any hurry in its measurement of her assigned time.

*   *

THEN suddenly it was Monday, the day the Calovattos were to leave. Downstairs the other evening Mary Calovatto had said, "The Plentaggers are going to drive Giulio and I to our plane at J.F.K." Elaine had had a restless night and had arisen early and was taking a walk under the trees in the square. As she swung to the edge of the loop toward Academy Street, she saw Mary Calovatto and Merle Plentagger walking up the sidewalk with packages in their arms. Mrs. Calovatto was looking brand new in her semitropical Ionojet slacks suit—very daring, Elaine thought, for a skirty woman. Elaine ran across the grass to the iron railing and called out, "Mary! Hey, Mary! You look great! Have a wonderful trip!"

The women's faces whipped toward the source of the shout. Elaine saw them glance at each other for a moment. They scanned the sidewalk, up and down: there were three or four pedestrians going about their business. The two women ran very fast across the street toward Elaine, frowning up a hurricane.

At the railing they pulled up huffing, and Mrs. Calovatto said, with her teeth set close together and in a low voice, as if afraid of being overheard, "Listen, you dumb bitch."

Mrs. Plentagger said, also just above a whisper, "What do you think you are, the Columbia Broadcasting System?"

"What did I—"

Mrs. Plentagger: "Look, dummy. Wooster Square you don't announce your comings and goings."

Mrs. Calovatto: "In particular your goings. We don't advertise empty apartments."

Elaine: "I'm *sorry*. I was trying to be friendly."

Mrs. Calovatto, Elaine's friend: "Friendly isn't such a big mouth."

*   *

Elaine kept walking her black-and-blue self-esteem around and around under the sycamores, oaks, and elms. At about ten o'clock she saw Giulio Calovatto and Homer Plentagger emerge from the house carrying between them a very large cardboard carton, of the sort movers use to carry hanging clothes. It was almost as big as a coffin. They went north on Academy and turned east on Greene at the top of the square. At the far corner, nearly to Wooster Place, they came to the Plentaggers' Torino station wagon. Elaine wondered why it was parked so far from the house; there was plenty of parking space right in front of it. The men put the carton down on the sidewalk. They seemed nervous. Plentagger unlocked his car. Two people were walking past. The men waited until the two were well down the street, checked to see that no one else was coming, quickly opened the flap of the carton, extracted from it two suitcases, put them in the back of the station wagon, then took from the carton a large piece of canvas, which they spread over the suitcases, evidently to hide them. Then they locked the car and hurriedly carried the carton back to the house. Five minutes later the Calovattos came out of the house and walked south on Academy. A little after that the Plentaggers came out and walked north, turned right, went to their car, and drove down Greene and out of the Square toward Olive Street. Elaine watched the Calovattos turn left on Chapel Street at the foot of the square, and pretty soon here came the Torino back the other way, down on Chapel. It stopped. The Calovattos jumped in. The car went on.

A knock in the rhythm of *Shave and a haircut, two bits.* Repeated, louder.

Elaine looked at her watch. Nine thirty-five. She was rocking and reading "A Good Man Is Hard to Find." The Misfit had just taken Elaine's breath away by shooting the grandmother. She hesitated. Should she answer the door at all? Then she realized the record player was going; she could scarcely pretend she was out.

She went to the door and opened it. Homer Plentagger in a seedy terrycloth bathrobe and nothing else. Oh, God, she thought, this specimen is going to examine my terrariums and then take a lunge at me.

"Miss Quinlan?" he asked, as if he wanted to be sure he could believe his eyes.

"*I* saw your getaway this morning," Elaine said, brightly blinking. "You didn't fool *me*."

But: "Would you please turn the music down? *Working* people"—the crying shame of unemployment shook in his adam's apple—"have to get some sleep."

"Oh. You're right under me, aren't you?"

"It's not just us," Mr. Pesticides said. "Giulio tells me he hasn't been able to get a wink ever since you moved in."

"He'll get caught up under a tropic moon."

Mr. Plentagger tightened the belt of his bathrobe with a sudden tug. "I understand you have a bit to learn about shouting in the streets around this neighborhood."

"Is it really that bad?"

"Don't come running to *me* with your throat cut," he said, and turned on his bare tootsies and went downstairs.

Chapter 7

Macaboy is at his workbench, and in the flow of his rituals he might be a priest at an altar, except that he hasn't a stitch of clothing on. There is an early June heat wave. His skin glistens like a space suit. His balls are drawn up tight with work.

He is making a flush door. This is to be the Prince of Doors. A pure door, an essence. First principle: *Plywood sucks.* Second law: *Veneer is Nixonian—all cover-up.* The door is being joined from the pieces of aged two-inch walnut that Macaboy chose at Medary's, which will face the eye of the beholder as naked as Macaboy was at birth and is now. The door will be heavy in the best sense, like the facial expressions of Humphrey Bogart—tough, authentic, mysterious. Its design will follow a classic tradition: the stiles and rails are already trimmed, mortised, and tenoned, and slender wedges to lock the tenons lie ready on a tray on the bench, like slivers cut from a small wheel of cheese and laid out for drink time. There will be an extra rail at the waist, so there will be upper and lower panels. But these are to be as thick as their frame—it will be a *flush* door, as safe as Hoover Dam— and the beauty will be in the dance of grains, not in the play of highlights that comes from piling on frills. There'll be none of your whorish bevels or molding, no panel freak's chamfers or astragals or bolections or cocked beads. Just one perfect surface on which the statements of nature will fill the eye, as they do in a seascape. But this great simplicity calls for precisions as confining as those of certain great complexities on which human life hangs, such as microcentimetrically tolerant Rolls-Royce airplane engines, and this afternoon's task may be the most exacting of all. He is gluing up the upper panel: six slim hexahedrons to be forced together, perfectly squared, without the least winding or washboarding— flat as a sheet of plate glass.

For a benchmark Macaboy now puts Mozart's *Symphonia Concertante* on the record player; this entire door will have been built to Mozart. Baroque music as a conscience for the sculptor of a bare plane? Macaboy sees it this way: The fluency of genius (read: "energy," or E) equals mc^2, where m is the material, namely two-inch walnut, and c is cock-pride—or cunt-pride, it would be, if the carpenter were of another sort. It is in the squaring of that c—not easy on this earth—that high achievement for the merely talented must lie.

Now he goes in the kitchenette, sets the water for his gluepot on the stove, turns a knob, and licks at the fart of natural gas with a butane-gas cigarette lighter. The burner ignites with a *fffut*. For Macaboy uses good old-fashioned hot animal glue. None of your epoxies, thank you. In the screed of the headlong rush to entropy, let it be written that Macaboy at least used biodegradable materials.

He returns to the bench to check the six splines of the panel one last time. These pieces, each $38'' \times 3\frac{5}{8}'' \times 1\frac{7}{8}''$, are leaning against the bench. Using a two-foot-long wooden block plane, he has shot them true along their edges in pairs, so that any slight deviations from the square in his work will be compensated, because the paired edges will fit these deviations exactly together. He has matched the grains, alternated the heart sides, and had a dream of the portals of the Baths of Caracalla: Macaboy recognizes a smarmy grandeur of scale in his visions.

He draws wooden horses from under the bench, sets up three long metal carpenter's clamps across them, and with a spirit level and some almost paper-thin hardwood shives brings the clamps into a sweet unanimous horizontality. He lays the splines out on these clamps in the proper order; props against the bench, in readiness, two other clamps, which will be placed face down on the splines to hold them flat; and arranges on the edge of the workbench the stubs of waste wood he will use to protect the outer edges of the panel from being bruised by the clamps when he gives them their urgency.

In all his movements there is an ocelot caution. He sometimes wonders himself: What is the prey he is stalking?

A SHORT wait, now, for the gluepot to heat up. He goes to the phone, lifts the horn, flicks his finger roundly seven times with a kind of impatient ferocity, like that of a powerful businessman, and listens.

"Helena Beadle Real Estate."

He disguises his voice. "Good afternoon. Do you have any listings, out like on St. Ronan Street, around there, of rabbit hutches? I was thinking of doing some breeding."

"Silly."

"How did you know it was me?"

"You're about as good of an actor as James Stewart."

"Thanks a mil."

"What do you want, Fast Eddie, more scaredycat ladies?"

"Don't *call* me that."

"What about that last one I gave you? She sounded right up your alley."

"She wasn't interested. Tell you about her when I see you."

"Such as when? Hey. *Clockwork Orange*. Tonight?"

"Yeah. Yeah. I do want to see that. Tonight? Sure."

"Which showing?"

"Depends. You want to do it before or after? It's usually real good after—specially after these movies with gang bangs in them. You know? You see all that slightly speeded-up film, then you can go home and haul ashes. Keen!"

"Eddie!"

"Yes, missy. So solly."

"Come on, man. I thought we had a business relationship."

"Look. I'm working on a champion door. Why don't you just come over when you shut up shop, and after I'm finished we can go to Rudy's and then take in the flicker. O.K.?"

"If you'll at least put on a pair of pants before I arrive."

"You know me inside and out, don't you?"

"I know the out. I have it memorized. I don't have to see it again . . . I don't think I'll ever know the in."

DIPPING the glue from the pot and brushing it on always starts him reeling off some passage of noninstant replay. That viscid, opalescent, hot, sticky stuff—it might be a pot of jism. Ten trillion comings: what a way to get a bond! This time, mating the splines of the door panel—a groupie happening of sorts—he revisits the strangest period of all, the phase of euphoria and explosive sexuality and total generosity the Oregon group went through just after the Four Days of Rage. Almost everyone had been to Chicago. You wore a dirty gauze bandage wound around your cracked head for ten days as if it were Admiral Nelson's boss hat. *Smash monogamy!* was the cry. (He rubs the two prepared splines together until, as carpenters say, they suck.) *Before we build a new society we have to destroy the shit in each and every one of us.* The gut-check sessions were fantastic. Everything had mellowed. Even the guy Macaboy liked the least, Dandy Hartwohl, was less of a viper than usual. People touched each other all the time: men women, men men, women women. Are you revolutionary enough to tear down every vestige of bourgeois uptightness? Can you really get to know your own body connections, headbone to neckbone, cockbone to hipbone? Can you accept homo along with hetero? Can you give up doing dope—well, for a week? Seen now, with a lift of this brush dripping with hot seminal goo, the entire phase was one in which everybody, women included, went ape-shit for every known mode of male penetration. All the words to describe the new consciousness had behind them the thrust of an erection: pushy, hard, driving, determined, energetic. Nail 'em up against the wall! It was a wild upper, like getting your first driving license: you had a license to fuck: literally and in mind-boggling metaphors.

He is ready to take up the clamps. The jism is still warm between the wooden thighs. The name Melissa Ezqueidar comes into his mind, and suddenly this hard-eyed, meticulous, bare-assed craftsman, leaning over to turn a metal crank, feels a *blush* climb from his neck onto the balconies of his cheeks. Melissa Ezqueidar was sixteen. She had run away from home—Alabama Avenue, Indianapolis, Indiana. She had hitched to L.A., with a head full of movie-magazine fantasies, and then like the whales offshore began drifting north along the coast on compelling currents. She wound up staying, with written permission from her mother, in Home Port, in Portland, a house for teeny-bopper crazies and runaways that some revolutionaries had got clean official papers for. Her mother, of Norwegian descent, was a checkout lady in a Safeway store. Her father, a wild-talking Basque lumber fork-lift driver, had everlastingly yearned for the sea and had maintained a bowling average of 192 until he was drafted and exported and killed near Lon Nai—so Melissa told Macaboy the first night they talked. Melissa was an all-American sweetie. As a sophomore in high school, the year before, she had been co-captain of the pep squad and had joined Future Nurses of America. She liked Little Richard and Johnny Cash. She left home plainly and simply because after her father was killed her mother gave her the willies. The people who ran Home Port brought her to a self-criticism session of Macaboy's collective, thinking the group might become a new family for her. She sat opposite Macaboy in a soiled miniskirt. The skin of her neck, when she pulled her hair out from her cheek, running her fingers right out to the ends, looked delicate and overripe, like a slightly brown-turned petal of a white carnation that wished it had been pink. The insides of her thighs were like margarine—yellowish and, it seemed to Macaboy, spreadable. Right after the meeting Macaboy took responsibility for raising Melissa's consciousness. She was so interested in political theory that she accepted the second part of the lecture upstairs, on her back, with her teacher on top of her. She trembled violently, and Macaboy thought: *This chick has problems.* Her main problem soon came surfing forth on the curl of a wave of tears: this son of a bitch had just split her maidenhead. She raved for several hours, keening most of her threnody not at Macaboy, whom she addressed exclusively as *you ferking shithead*, but at her dear dead daddy. The next day at Home Port she took all her clothes off, wrapped herself in the American flag that had been given her the previous year, neatly folded after its removal from her father's coffin, and ran through the streets of Portland, with the little triangle of her pubis winking now and then from under the stars and stripes, shrieking, "Murderers! Murderers! Murderers!" The city police, their nerves hyperfrazzled after a series of radical student pranks, caught up with her at the corner of Freemont and Fifteenth, and gave her a demonstration of nightstickery which entailed, as a sequel, late that night, an announcement to the press from the authorities at Good Samaritan Hospital: "The patient's condition has stabilized. Her life signs are returning to normal."

MACABOY and Liz Roecake are back again at Rudy's, after the movie. The glass surface of the pitcher of beer between them is sweating out the interminable post-mortem of yet another brace of moviegoers.

Liz took a course in film criticism at Mount Holyoke. "Kubrick," she is saying, "has to have the clearest eye of any director ever. All that whiteness—perfect for a color film.

White's a reflection of all the colors of the spectrum. It's the all-color of evil, huh? Huh? Like why was Moby Dick a *white* whale?"

"Too easy," Macaboy gloomily says. "This guy Kubrick has gross dreams. The son of a bitch makes his victims evil. That writer, that upper-class dame. The sadist comes out the only human being you can empathize with. Shit."

"Oh, but the way he can make you *feel* Alex's face in those close-ups. Couldn't you just reach out and *touch* him?" Ms. Roecake has her hands up, left higher than right, aiming a pretend hand-held camera at the pores on Macaboy's neck.

"Beyond a certain point, technique gets to be dehumanizing in itself. I've been thinking about this. We got so we concentrated on the tactics of a protest . . ."

"_____?"

"There was a turning point in the Movement," he says. "We all got so we had those clear Kubrick eyes you were talking about. Everything looked white white white. I've been trying . . ." His voice trails off.

"Oh, God," Liz says, feeling slippage in her film-criticism career. "Not that ancient history again."

Macaboy stares into his beer glass.

"You're a case," Liz says.

"I'm sorry." He is back on the scene, his smile is dear. "What were you saying?"

"I was—"

"Hey, that client on Academy Street I was going to tell you about. Hoo, Lizzy-baby, you should hear her voice! Velvet underground!"

"But you said she turned you down."

"Not for long. She'll call. I planted the seed."

"I wish I knew what you want from me."

H E walks Roecake to the door of her apartment on York, then strolls down Chapel away from home. There is some-

thing contained, concentrated, pressurized about his hiproll
and kneeflex as he glides down the sidewalk; he seems guided
by the servos of a single hypered sense, like a field-ranging
retriever informed by the radar buzzing off its nose end. Another pedestrian might think that this automated steering
apparatus is heading Macaboy toward the Grove Street
whores, who hang around outside the porno houses like
striped bass lying off tide-pool estuaries—chippies who, because of the way their clientele have been psyched by the
films, get a heavy business in what is called in the trade oral
hygiene. But no, that is not his choice. He doesn't turn on
College. He goes straight down. The Green is to his left. On
it, the medieval gloom of Trinity Church is pricked out by
the lights of commerce across the way. He thinks of his
mother dressed for church. She is wearing white cotton
gloves, she has a habit of tapping the fingers of her left hand
on the back of her right hand. The wax cherries on her hat
vibrate with her jaw motions. She's a talker. Bang, the memory of his mistake in putting fine chicken wire on the front of
a wooden Carnation Condensed Milk box as a cage for his
white mice. They easily gnawed a hole through the thin
wood and got out. Found Mother's hat. Ate the wax cherries
right down to the wire stems. From that day onward Mother
disapproved of *everything he did*. He has a slight, not un-
pleasant ache in his chest as he walks. Now all of a sudden he
says to himself, "Well, Jesu, what do you know? Academy
Street! How did I get *here?*"

He walks left on Academy, on the built-up side. The woods
in the square across the way are dark, as in the beginning of a
Grimm brothers' tale. Number 32 is about three-quarters of
the way up the square, not far beyond Court Street. It is a big
cube in the Italian-Villa style, fancied forth with a central
pediment—sheathed, however, in most un-Italian clapboard.
By the light of a sputtering street lamp Macaboy contem-
plates the ornamented window trim—workmanship, he can
tell even in the dark, that would be out of the question today.

There are nine windows on the façade, three of them tucked up under the bold Tuscan eaves. He wonders . . .

He turns and floats away toward his apartment.

THIS time he does not bother to pick his lock; he uses a key. Inside he peels off his shirt and lets it flutter to the floor. With a finger he tests one of the beads of glue between the splines of the door panel. Perfect. The glue is firm yet rubbery. It will cut easily without smearing and is not so set as to crimp a tempered-steel edge. He sharpens a chisel and trims the beads wherever he can without loosening the clamps. Opens a bottle of beer. Flops on his bed. Picks up *Nostromo* and reads. Falls asleep, against his own will, as Nostromo and Decoud are crossing the gulf in the night on their lighter loaded with bars of silver.

Chapter 8

PeOPLE change, Elaine decided.

"Have some more sangría!" Bottsy Feldman shouted. She told Elaine she had mixed this gore herself. She was on the third chapter of her dissertation on Peter Kropotkin. Her Lake Place room was a slaughterhouse of literary materials: broken-spined books, slashed leaves of Xerography, pages and pages of crossed-out longhand, all over desk and bed and floor. It was as if this red sangría of hers had been made from the blood of the body of Western learning.

"No, thanks, no more right now," Elaine said.

"Have you read Kropotkin?"

"No, I haven't. I've heard of him, of course."

Elaine knew at once that that little lie, told out of an innocent wish to be acceptable, was a booby trap, and she knew, too, who the born booby was. Bottsy went on and on. Elaine weaved her questions around her delicate but finally inescapable condition of ignorance about this Kropotkin of Bottsy's. Bottsy called him Pyotr Alekseyevich in husky tones as if he were her lover. Bottsy had grown a bit butchy. As a boy Pyotr Alekseyevich was a page to the Czar. That much came out. It didn't help.

Elaine was thinking of the spottiness of her Bennington

gleanings. She had been certified as educated, with a Bachelor of Arts degree from an accredited institution of higher learning, without having taken a single course in math beyond algebra, or in physics, chemistry, biology, geology, astronomy, archaeology, or anthropology, or econ or poli sci. She had been a whiz in Russian. She had picked up a smattering of Sanskrit, now totally wiped out. As a junior she had been up to her nates in psych and then been turned off by Professor Ouda, who was into feelies, particularly of nates. Then she finally got on a proper Bennington kick—architectural design. What griped her now was that all her Slavic studies hadn't told her Word One about this Pyotr Alekseyevich.

There was a puzzling reference to a lecture Kropotkin gave at Wellesley. Bottsy let it out of the bag that French workingmen called him *"notre Pierre."* The great gesture of dropping his Russian princely title!

Elaine felt that she was getting warm, but at this point Bottsy kicked off her shoes and began to cry.

Elaine was fascinated by Bottsy's bare feet. How stubborn they were! They were chunky, with short, fat, blunt toes. Tears fell on them.

At Bennington, Bottsy had been winsome, compactly put together, and neat fun. She had majored in studio art. Sang folk songs with sweet thin oboe reeds in her neck. She had seemed to be rich. She had flapped around, as carefree as a catbird. Elaine had never seen her bare feet at Bennington.

First there had been Ruth Greenhelge, transformed. Now Bottsy. Everyone changed except Elaine Quinlan.

Elaine wanted to comfort Bottsy somehow. Showing an evasive interest in Kropotkin had apparently not been helpful. "Want to hear about my first job interview in New Haven, Connecticut?" she asked.

Bottsy snuffled and pushed at her nose with her thick forearm.

"Charter Oak Bank," Elaine said. "I didn't get the job."

"God how I wish I could work in a bank," Bottsy burst

out. "I'd do *stenography*. I'd sit on the boss's *lap*. Anything!"
She began to cry again.

Elaine wanted to say, "You can't change back into what
you were before," but instead she said, "Oh, I can do short-
hand, old Botts. Pitman system. Three hundred words a
minute. I bet you thought I'd been wasting my time all these
years." Elaine felt a tiny push of malice. Where did Bottsy
Feldman get off, thinking the spilt milk of this world was all
hers?

"The old twot in the personnel office asked me about
schooling, and the moment I said Bennington College I saw a
teeny gate close in her eyes, and I knew she was going to hand
me a douche bag. 'I'm afraid you're overqualified, my dear.' "
Elaine talked through the personnel woman's nose, which
was overdue for a defrosting. "I know what I should have
said. I should have said, 'It's O.K., Miss Bubblegum. I didn't
learn zilch at Bennington College. I'm dumb enough to do a
real dumb job'—that's what I should have said. I should have
asked her, 'Haven't you got any *real* dumb jobs?' "

Bottsy looked suddenly cheerful: her eyes were dry, and
her teeth looked like the keyboard of a not-brand-new ac-
cordion. "You always did run yourself down," she said. "It
was a way you had of making the rest of us seem conceited.
Or masculine. Maybe you wanted us to look masculine. That
it?"

You could have played a pretty tune on Bottsy Feldman's
smile.

Justy was blocking her way on the stairs. Elaine stood
with a heavy grocery bag in each arm, waiting for him to
move aside. Her back ached. He was sweeping the steps without seeming to touch the broom to them, as if the stairs had a
fever and needed to be fanned. She cleared her throat. He
turned full around in two slow clicks. Signs of pleasure
spread on his face from the nose outward. The whopped jaw

gaped into a twisted grimace of sweet recognition and defer-
ence.

"Could I get by?"

"Oh, yes'm, Missus Quillan. Come ahead."

Click click click. But there was not room to pass.

He was propping the broom against the wall of the stair-
well. "Hep you carry them bundles," he said.

"No thanks, Justy," she said. "I'm all balanced."

She was trying to push past. His arms reached out. She
dropped down one step. "Here," he said. "Give me this." For
a blurred second she thought he had said: *Give me a kiss.*
The back of his hand pressed her left breast. She began to
fight for her life. His will was strong. She felt her heart ac-
celerate. She heard the start of a paper-tearing sound. Then
he had wrenched the bag from her grasp and—*click, click,
click*—he turned with creaks and moans of effort and went
slowly up ahead of her, the machinery in his pants hinging
and unhinging.

In the kitchen she thanked him, saying he was very kind,
and to confirm what she had said he aimed the full blast of
his awareness of his kindness from his eyes to hers. She hated
herself for moving so as to put the kitchen table between him
and herself, and she began at once to take things out of the
bags. Justy stood his ground. "If you'll excuse me," she said,
beginning to be frightened by her fear. Then she heard him
clicking off. "I'm a fucking racist," she thought.

S HE went walking in the park at sunset. She had begun to
wonder whether she should call Greg. His laughter kept
bouncing around in her head, like the barking of dogs on a
full-moon night. She strolled south toward Columbus. Suddenly, as if she were swimming up from sleep, she realized
something was—there was a man looming over her in the
flickering shade, and she felt a leap of panic. He was tall,

grizzly. The face was haggard, the eyes burned with lust. It was Homer Plentagger. She made a quick adjustment: those were *not* the embers of lust, he just looked dangerously friendly. "I saw you walking," he said. "We got a card from Mary Calovatto. She said, 'Say hello to the girl in second-floor-back.' "

"Fantastic," Elaine said, surprised by the shock of delight this message had given her, even though it seemed Mrs. Calovatto had forgotten her name. "Are they having fun?"

"Yeah," the pesticides man said, beaming down on her like a spray can. "Yeah. That's just what she said. Having fun."

"Wish we were there," Elaine said, to make a little joke in postcardese.

But that "we" may have been a mistake. Mr. Plentagger turned to walk along beside her, and with a new stab of fear she divined that he would ask about her terrariums. He would want to look them over. He would show up in that seedy terrycloth bathrobe. He would stand in the hall and flash the wings of the robe open, and there would be nothing underneath but a ragged carrot, its curly foliage lightly dusted with insect repellent.

"What would Mrs. Plentagger think," Elaine asked, as demurely as possible, "if she knew that hubbykins was walking in the park with a girl half his age?"

"Merle?" Pesticides guffawed, and Elaine thought she could see clouds of Lindane and Captan and what was his own patented death powder?—Supalgran?—billowing forth from the regions of his uvula. "She could care less."

He raised a hand to scratch an ear. It was, Elaine saw, a surprisingly strong hand, full-muscled between thumb and forefinger, with black hairs from knuckle to knuckle. She was aware of goosebumps on her buttocks and a queer dissolved feeling in her abdomen. And she knew she was angry—but she didn't know exactly at what—perhaps at Greg. She would never go back. Never. She would stay right here. And get a job. And change—for the better, unlike Greenie and Bottsy.

She hardly noticed, near the statue of Columbus, that Mr. Plentagger had peeled off.

THE telephone was sitting there on the floor, like a black turtle, beside the rocking chair. She knew it had a bell in its bowels. How strange! She had forgotten Greg's number—her own number for so long. An hour ago she had gone to the notebook that she kept in her small tin strongbox with her junk jewelry, and had looked the number up. She had written it on a torn slip of paper with a green felt pen. The slip was on the floor next to the phone. The notation looked like flecks of dried seaweed. She rocked. Once in a while she looked at the seaweed. She could not seem to move anything but her pushing foot and leg. She was in warm water and a strong hand with hair between the joints of the fingers was sliding along her flank. . . .

She woke with a headache and blundered to bed, where she lay awake, waiting for something to happen, until the window rectangle was gray; then she fell into a dreamstorm of a nap.

SHE woke a little after eleven and went right to the phone.

"Is this Helena Beadle?"

"It is." Elaine could *see* the hips in that voice.

"This is Elaine Quinlan. You found me this apartment on Wooster Square?"

"Yes, dear. I hope everything's *così così*."

"It's fine. Except. I gather from the other people in the house that the security here isn't so good. I was wondering. Do you happen to know of a locks—?"

"Did you lose your keys, honey? We all do that when we first move in. I don't know, maybe Freud—or Jung—my friends all say Jung is—maybe Jung has an explanation. Never fails."

"No, I just—"

"I've been in this business twenty-eight years. Never fails."

Elaine decided not to try to explain why she was calling; she didn't know whether she could make her reasons clear to herself. "I wondered if you—"

"My Girl Friday knows of one. We've had to, on account of this—"

"Your girl *who?*"

"Just an expression, darling." Aside: "Liz, what's the number of that locksmith we keep recommending?" Pause. "Got a pencil, honey? Three six five. Four two oh seven. The name is peculiar—you have to spell it out. S-a-f-e-hyphen-capital-T . . ."

"Oh, no."

The Beadle continued spelling.

"Are you sure? They're reliable? I got a bad phone call from them."

"We get raves from people. Absolute raves. They're out of this world."

"Are they trustworthy?"

"Honey, they're like the First National Bank."

"Well. . . . If you say so."

"SAFE-T Securit-E Syst-M!"

"Hello, this is—"

"Oh *hello,* Mzz Quinlan. We've been expecting your call."

Long pause.

"Could you send someone to change the tumbler, or cylinder, whatever, in my lock?"

"Indeed. Indeed. May I ask what type lock it is?"

"I'll have to look." Sound of footsteps. "Yale. What else, in this burg?"

"Yale, we have Yale. When would be convenient?"

"This afternoon? . . . Like say two o'clock?"

"Very *good*."

"Will you send somebody who's . . . I mean, the telephone people sent this incredible creep to install—"

"All our people are bonded, Mzz Quinlan. Let's see. We'll send this young fellow, Eddie. He's a mechanical genius— really—and a nice gentle person in the bargain. Very good-looking. He's tall, wears this ponytail effect . . ."

"Look, mister, I want a lock installed, I don't want a call-boy."

Chapter 9

THERE is no form of flying for Macaboy that is higher in the sky than his joy in the clean fielding of door panels. The panels are to be let into the frame with rabbets: these will give the door the integrity, from the outside, of a bank vault. And of all the operations in joining, what sweeter and prouder one than rabbeting well across the end of the grain? Macaboy has sharpened the little gossipy tongue of the spur of his rebate plane, has set the width fence and the depth stop, and has let down the razor-edged cutter only so much as would barely peel away that atomic skin of a body of water which is called surface tension. He starts with utmost care at the far end, with caressing strokes allowing the spur, first, to define the width of the rabbet without breaking away any grain ends, then whispering the *so*-sharp cutter with goose-down strokes along the full width of the channel—seven-eighths of an inch—and off the end with never a fiber carried away. Now he gradually works backward, still with short air-weight strokes, until he has started the work on the whole edge; after that he shoots the entire length of the cut with even, light runs of the blade that have the sound of faraway skis schussing on corn snow. A light dry dust comes away. He stops now and then to take out the cutter blade and whet it, honing the edge on the oilstone until it is as keen and biting as the mind of Joseph Conrad—for Macaboy, who has seen many places, thinks he has never had pictures cut so sharply into his mind as are those of the wholly imaginary landscape of Costaguana he was reading about last night. He reinserts the tongue and goes back to work. Each stroke requires two soft-padded ocelot steps along beside the upended panel.

B-r-r-r-i-n-g-g-g!

With the reflex of a man who has touched the fierce heat of dry ice, Macaboy jerks the plane away from the wood: It is his instinct, when an alarm sounds, to save the artifact first and then look to his own skin. But it is only the phone. He takes the black box onto the bed.

"Safe-T Securit-E Syst-M!"

"Hello, this is—"

"Oh, *hello,* Mzz Quinlan. We've been expecting your call."

Macaboy has read of Oriental mystics who have learned to regulate their pulse rate and blood pressure by processes of meditation, and while planing, even in his daydream of Costaguana, Macaboy has managed for the sake of absolute steadiness of hand to approach their level of control. It is therefore all the more noticeable to him that the governor of his fuel pump has now suddenly gone haywire. He cannot seem to command his tongue to explain to the client why "tumbler" is wrong; he senses, as part of the blurred landscape shooting past the window of this rushing train, a lame joke about Yale locks and New Haven, but it is gone by before he realizes what it was. The important thing is to fix a time. *Today*—the client suggests—*two o'clock.* He must remember. Considering his lack of focus he describes rather well the person who is to be sent.

THEN it is all over. His mind is fuzzy, his brain has grown gray fur, like bread left too long in the breadbox. What time did the client suggest? He really can't recall. Early afternoon? *Two? Three?* Should he go at two thirty to be safe?

He goes back to the bench, picks up the plane. One shot along the rabbet channel tells him he must stop and wait for a better time. The grain seems to have turned hummocky; his unsteady hand sings with a vibrato.

S HE swings the door open.

He turns his back to her, so she can read the legend on his blue twill coverall.

"You're the locksmith."

He waves a yellow work order in his hand. "Forgive me, the office gave me—the name was—?"

"Elaine Quinlan."

"Just making sure I have the right door." He does not bounce a name back but points to the cursive *Eddie* on his breast pocket.

"May I survey the layout?"

"Be my guest."

He steps inside, takes the doorknob, and clicks the door shut. They are closed into the room together with the door locked. She moves away, to the other side of a rocking chair. But then he is on his knees, squinting at the poor fit of door to jamb, of latch to strike plate. He wobbles the knob, which is loose in its seating. He stands, opens the door again, taps the jamb and trim with the knuckle of his middle finger, and turns to her.

This is the first time he has fired his high-energy look at her. "Ah," he says. Is this a professional statement?

Her neck is longish, and as she stands now there is a curve of her spine and a slight tilt of her head like those of a figure by Correggio: one of the paintings that hit him so hard in Parma. She has hung an orange-colored poster on the wall to her right, and her cheek on that side, reflecting its glow, looks like cantaloupe meat at the prime of readiness. Her eyes, greenish blue, have splinters of yellow suspicion in them. Her shoulders are full, she holds her hands flat as if ready to deliver a chop with a curdling outcry. Is that eye shadow on her lids, or the bluish transparency that follows shallow sleep broken into by fitful dreams of biting dogs and of struggles to reach destinations? Her hostile eyes are on his, so he chooses not to look at her breasts. Somewhere in the ribcage behind them is the seat of that voice, which now sounds: "So?"

"The doorframe," he says, "is like Aetna Life. They don't make 'em like that any more. But this door." He shakes his head.

At the moment she has nothing to say.

"That door is about as much protection as a potato pancake."

He sees ground glass in the blue-green irises, so he softens his tone. "See, they must have replaced the original—who knows when? The problems you have: These panels—cheapshit plywood, corrugated cardboard would be just as good. Then you have this Grand Canyon between the edge of the door and the jamb; makes for a totally unsafe situation: jimmying's far too easy. On top of that you have one of these tinsel knob locks. Our company is kind of old-fashioned, we much prefer a mortised lock. Look at this loose knob, anyhow." He rattles it again.

"You finished?"

"The hinges—"

"Pack it in, sonny. I asked for a key change."

"Sure. Sure. I brought a Yale cylinder. I just thought—"

"Sometimes a person can think too much—like right over the edge."

"We'll fix you right up, Miss Quinlan." What a slash, to go from Mzz to Miss! Her eyes catch it. He turns and begins rattling around in his wooden tool box. He is charming. While he works he talks—croons. This section, Wooster Square, used to be Little Italy. The church across the square, St. Michael's. You wouldn't be apt to see Renaissance churches like that in Rome or Florence—it is more a small-town type of church. Yeah. (The "yeah" is in response to a question that should have been asked but hasn't been.) Did a hitching trip through Italy and North Africa two years ago. You might think of your average church as being open to worshipers twenty-four hours a day. Not in Popesville. Santa Maria in Trastevere, old part of Rome, you have these iron-work gates to the portico—fantastic mosaics—iron fence must be twenty feet high to keep the sacred-vessel snatchers out. "I mean," he says, "security is a very pervasive concept." The keys to those iron gates, at a conservative estimate: eight inches long. But these kids play soccer in the square in front of the church, and all the time some hero keeps kicking the ball over the top. You ought to see them climb over that twenty-foot fence—spikes at the top! Those kids could rob the Virgin Mary blind.

She hovers. It is not that she hangs back. She seems interested in the work and part of the time leans over his shoulder to watch. He is on his knees. Once or twice he imagines he feels her breath on his neck. This operation usually takes no more than five minutes. He prolongs it with numerous false moves—most enjoyable when working under such close scrutiny.

Until a guy named Mayor Lee came along, he says, Wooster Square was a slum. The Eyeties came in in the nineties—immigrants. Before that this section was called the New Township: all kinds of prosperity. These are elegant houses. People don't even *look* at them.

"I do," she says in a suddenly friendly voice. "I was thinking at one time of going into architecture."

"A woman architect," he says. "There aren't too many. They say architecture calls for a really autocratic temperament."

No response.

For a while, this was really the heart of New Haven. Down here, he says, along Mill River, things hummed. Brewster carriage factory. Clocks, bentwood chairs, rubber boots, hardware, melodeons, daguerreotypes. "Our company requires its operatives to know this city cold."

She is silent.

"I see you're a reader," he says.

She says nothing. His fingers keep twiddling.

"My favorite is *The Charterhouse of Parma*. Did you ever read *The Charterhouse of Parma*?"

"Modern European lit," she says. "Junior year."

"Stendhal wrote that mother in fourteen weeks, can you believe it? The part where Fabrizio is locked up in the tower —this totally visual love affair he carries on! That really sends me."

She says nothing. Twiddle-diddle delay. He is running out of tactics.

"Junior year? Where?"

"Bennington."

"Holy shit. You one of those?"

"What is that supposed to mean?"

"I don't know, Bennington chicks, there's something so— they're like Mondrians. Or *imitation* Mondrians. Very hard-edged. Patterned. Know what I mean? I went west to college."

"Are you almost done?" The voice is like a paring knife.

"Almost." His knees on the hardwood floor feel as if they were stuffed with damp peat moss. "Sometimes," he says, "I think words—I mean *spoken* words, print is something else— words that we speak are poor tools. I like to use good tools." He shakes a magnetized screwdriver at her over his shoulder. "One thing I never learned in college was how to say what I mean. I can *think* all these things perfectly, but like when it comes to pushing those thoughts over into sound—I don't know." He rises, almost bumping into her. "Do you think it's just us?"

"Us?" she sharply asks, as if he has made an indecent proposal.

"People like us. My father never had any trouble finding accurate words—specially when I did something he didn't like. Here are your keys," he says. "Don't leave them lying around."

She reaches out a flat palm, and he drops the keys into it.

He is almost issuing beeps, his capacitors are so overloaded. "What I mean is, there never seems to be time to think out what you want to say. Then you spend a lot of time when it's too late trying to figure out what you would have said if you'd had time. Even then, the words are sort of—I don't know. Ever break a thermometer? It's ruined anyway, so you start playing with the little balls of mercury that spilled out? Words—am I—"

"How much?"

"Excuse me?"

"How much do I owe you?"

"The company doesn't charge for a first visit—if it's just a key change."

"Oh, man—"

"The company wants you to feel safe."

"You're putting me on."

"Cross my heart." He runs his forefinger in an X over the *Eddie*. "Look, here's the work order." He takes the yellow slip out of his thigh pocket, spreads it on his left hand, and moves around beside her, his shoulder almost touching hers. The slip has *Safe-T Securit-E Syst-M* printed across the top, all right. This is a carbon copy. "Look here. N slash C. That means 'no charge' on anybody's voucher, right?"

"New Haven is some loony town," she says.

"We'll sock it to you when we hang the door," he says with a sweet expression.

"No way, Eddie boy," she says. This is the first time she has granted him an identity.

On the way out he wobbles the loose doorknob and sends her an electric-eye beam.

*   *

Wʌɴᴛ to see a goofy man? Look at Macaboy pumping his knees up Chapel. You'd think he was sail planing. He has a good hard mouth for whistling—this time it's *Fidelio*. Florestan is chained in Don Pizarro's subterranean dungeon. Here comes Leonore dressed as a man, to save him. Rapturously: *O namenlose Freude!* The timbre of Macaboy's whistling is thick, piercing—like a cardinal's song. Ludwig van Beethoven bounces in splashes of redbird echo off the plate-glass windows of Ann Taylor's smart shop; behind the half-mirroring glass, the mannequins look surprised at Macaboy's euphoria. Suddenly the music breaks off. Macaboy could kick himself for the way that line about the Mondrians popped out. She is hypersensitive; she seems to be in a phase of temporary repairs. He sees her melon cheek; the hair has been shampooed; the eyes are flashing with an anger which, he would be willing to bet his final buck, doesn't tell the truth about itself. Will she feel safe? The lips go out, pursed, as if to kiss the day, but instead begin again to peal out Macaboy's high.

Chapter 10

Elaine went next morning to the Koin-Kleen on Orange Street.

Keeping George Washington sunnyside up, she put a dollar bill in the change machine. It was always a delightful surprise to her when the change came bursting out into its cup, as if she had hit at least two cherries and a bell on a one-armed bandit. The broken buck wouldn't last long. Thirty-five cents in the vending machine for a chinchy little box of Tide. Fifty cents for the washer: her sheets, pillowcase, and light fabrics were disposed around the agitator in one of the machines. The drier would chew up a nickel and a dime—and wouldn't get things beyond damp dry at that. First load. More to come.

"You're new here."

Elaine adored conversations in laundromats. Visits to laundromats were like plane rides: pickup relationships skirted to the very horizon of possibility and then quickly burned themselves out. Beyond the last tumble of the drier, as beyond the airport of destination, there could be no further claims.

"No," Elaine lied, "I just used to go to a laundromat over on Whalley. I've been in New Haven three long years."

The lady who had spoken was diagonally across from Elaine, shaking an appalling history of child rearing into a washer. The lady had a permanent wink in her right eye, with a matching droop of the right side of her mouth.

"Where do you live?"

"Lake Place," Elaine lied.

"Ooh, I wouldn't live there in a million years. They say they get burgled in there every night."

"My husband and I have been lucky," Elaine said, and she backed away to knock on the wood of a windowsill. "We haven't been broken into once."

" 'We'? You're such a pretty thing—I thought you was a student. A married woman?"

"Two years next week."

"But you have to be kidding me about your house. Everybody's been burgled. We been burgled three times, and we're on a good street—Lawrence."

"No, you see, we feel very secure. My husband is a locksmith. He knows how to safeguard a place."

"Bless Bob! Lucky you! What a gold mine, these days!"

"I suppose it could be, but my husband doesn't believe in ripping people off."

"What's the matter with his head, dearie? Everybody does it. How can he get any place?"

"He says, 'Why should I rob 'em? I'm trying to prevent their being robbed.' He's something else! Completely self-educated. He's the best-read person I know. He's reading Stendhal in French right now."

This was too embarrassing to discuss; the lady changed the subject. "No children, I see." She nodded toward Elaine's plastic laundry basket.

"I'm expecting."

"Oh, golly. How nice! It turns the world upside down, having little ones. When are you due?"

"Well, my doctor can't tell. The egg was lodged in the Fallopian tubes, and one of my husband's spermatozoa collared it in there, my uterus is tipped, and I have a very queer irritation from my vaginal deodorant."

The lady's one good eye did a loop-the-loop. "You got problems!"

SHE liked Greenhelge better this time. They went to The Blessings. Greenie knew how to order Peking food. They had six dishes. Greenie's fortune cookie said: CASH IS SLIPPING AWAY. REVIEW YOUR ACCOUNTING SYSTEM.

Greenie said, "You can say *that* again, Confucius."

They drank a gallon of tea and talked about parents.

Elaine said, "We had Dr. Spock all over the place. That was kind of remarkable for an Irish Catholic family. We never got spanked. I take it back: my brother was spanked *once*—with a soft, fuzzy slipper, and it sort of tickled his ass, and he laughed, and that pressed Father's potato-famine button, and he used the back of a hairbrush, for real. But that's absolutely the only time I can remember. Mostly—reasoning. Oh, God, they explained and explained and explained: we had to see every split hair of right and wrong. They were so *boringly* decent. Dad was in love with our Lab, Josephus. He was like St. Francis with that oaf of a hound. Mother, she was more of an amateur lawyer. What got her off was winning one for the good guys. She was always citing some decision of Justice Black or Learned Hand. They fell completely out of their tree over Stevenson. You could have cut the decency around our house with a hacksaw. And yet, when it came to each other: slam bang crash voom grrr pow—Jesus, Greenie, the fights! I mean, the crockery that got smashed. Real bruises, I *saw* them. One martini and—"

"Home, sweet home," Greenie said. "I had all that, too."

"Bet you didn't have this: After one of their championship bouts, Mom up and left—like I left Greg, come to think of it. She just packed up and popped me in the car and split. I was like eight. They couldn't get a divorce because of the Church.

Mom took a salt box near Montclair—her money. So one Sunday I'm out playing with a neighbor kid, and my Dad drives up, and he says, 'Hey, doll, want to go for a ride with Daddy? Hop in!' So sure, I get in, and he *kidnaps* me. Took me to Connecticut. He said he loved Mom and me so much he couldn't live without both of us."

"How did it come out?"

"Oh, hell, she followed us to Connecticut. Moved back in. I guess she'd really missed being slammed around."

Greenhelge said, "I've given up trying to use memories to account for the way I am."

"I don't think I'm going to get married," Elaine said. "I want to try to find the right guy, but I don't know, when you say 'till death us do part,' it clips your wings. It seems to shorten the time. I want the time to be long long long—and *varied*."

"But men want it on the line. They're always saying, 'Bottom line. Bottom line.' My boss is supposed to be a logician, he's married as you know, *he*'s always pawing me and talking about the bottom line. I *think* that means he wants me to sign a contract to fuck with no strings."

"You can get around that kind of junk."

"How?"

"Wiles, Greenie. Wiles. You've heard of wiles."

GREENHELGE drove Elaine to Wooster Square and dropped her in front of the house.

Elaine pushed the foyer door open, and in its rapid closing she thought she heard the rush of a hawk's wings. Then she realized that what she was actually hearing was music, and she froze: played the game of statues: one arm raised, one foot forward.

James Taylor was singing "Knocking Around the Zoo," loud for him, from the second floor. Back. The song was in the early album of his that she had. Elaine hovered there.

Should she go up at all? Greenie must have pulled away. She listened for a clicking sound mixed with the music, then remembered she had had the lock changed; the old master key would no longer work. She felt a blip of annoyance with the awkward young man from Safe-T Securit-E Syst-M—a lot of good he had done her! She reacted as she always did when she was conscious of the hawk—incautiously. She started up the stairs. Her crazy heart ran ahead of her.

She could see from the top of the flight that her door was standing wide open. The lights were on. Music was pouring out:

> *"Just knocking around the zoo on a Thursday afternoon*
> *There's bars on all the windows*
> *And they're counting up the spoons . . ."*

She paused beside the door to gather her recklessness together.

She walked in. Nothing. No one. Bright lights and loud music.

The bedroom. A light was shining in there, too.

She hugged herself. There was a motherly, protective love in her arms folded tight across under her breasts. The new Elaine—whenever she might arrive—was to have this tender side in good measure. It was a strength that was to come from a giving that was not to be a giving in.

Keeping her eye on her bedroom door, she went to the record player and shut it off. The abrupt silence was like an implosion, so powerful it might shatter the windows with its insucking force.

When the crash of the silence had passed, she loudly said (trying to drop her speech into the gut-sound of Bottsy Feldman's hoarse voice): "All right. Come on out."

She waited. Total silence. No clicks. No breathing. Hardly even her own.

"Justy?"

No answer.

"Who is it?"

No answer.

She stood like a fiberglass figure for a long, long time. Then she saw that one of her terrarium jars had been knocked from the mantel. She went to it. It was her artillery plant—when you reached in the jar and touched the clusters of blossoms with your fingertip they exploded into tiny clouds of pollen: if only all wars could be like that! The plant was fatally wounded. She knelt and mourned. The dirt and minifoliage and moss and glass had been gathered together into a heap on the floor. A slip of paper was beside the debris, and written on the paper in seaweed strokes were the words: REALLY SORRY. Her felt pen, its cap neatly replaced, lay beside the note.

She walked into the bedroom. At what she saw she whispered, "Jesus God!"

The room had been hit by a twister. The drawers were open. The bedcovers were pulled away. All her clothes were on the floor. The side tables were overturned. The lit lamp had fallen onto the bed. In the wild clutter she sensed an exuberance, a curiosity, a fierce appetite. She was drawn bodily into this indiscriminate energy and found herself standing—whirling—at the center of the room. Then she was suddenly still—as a Bernini statue, or Margot Fonteyn in repose, could be thought to be still, with massive kinetic energy trapped and trying to escape from the motionlessness—facing the open drawers. No. Not all her clothes were on the floor. Only her nightgowns, panties, bras, pantyhose. She stood among the pastel heaps, facing the dresser, and she saw the trajectories, the lines of flight of the flimsy texturized polyester-and-cottons and orlon acrylics and dacrons and polyurethanes, and old nylons and rayons she's never been able to bring herself to throw away, satinettes and fishnetweaves and linkstitches, everything skinsoft and sachet-sweetened that the old Elaine had folded into their places with such care—for this was a side of herself that no social pressure or ideology or even laziness could ever change—she'd gotten it from her goddam mother—she saw them all sucked out of the drawers in sudden jerks, up and out, then opening, parachuting, caressing the air, and in spasmodic ripples decelerating, the parabolas blunting as the airy stuffs fanned out, falling finally in crumpled limpnesses like stages of modesty torn off in haste and heedlessly dropped to the floor in a rush to nakedness and release in a bed whose covers have been flung back just as these had been, helter-skelter. She felt that she was being stripped naked. She saw the word *ripped* within the word *stripped.* Then she felt how cool the undy-freak's breath was on her—itself like the touch on her skin of a synthetic fabric. Perverse unwanted pleasure rose in her like a nausea and became one. She staggered toward the dark bathroom, thinking he might be in there—it didn't matter—and she made it and threw up, sweet and sour, hugging the toilet bowl as if it were the safe home of childhood games.

In time she was able to get up and wash her face. In the mirror: that old Elaine. Oh, God. She raised her hands and pushed that image away; turned, ran to the bedside, where she found the phone on the floor, the receiver sprawled away from its cradle, as if in a coma. She righted the side table and with trembling hands groped in its small drawer for her notebook. Found it, leafed, looked, dialed.

A deep voice: "This is your Supalgran man. Little plant pests hate me. If you—"

She banged the receiver down and dialed Greenhelge's number. No answer. At the core of her fear Elaine found a small shape crouching that looked like the beast of irony. Had Greenie taken her bellyful of moo goo gai pan awash with green tea to a tryst with the linguistics logician? In his office? The contract on his desk ready to sign? Oh, Greenie, Greenie, where is your revolution? Look at *me*, in *my* state of change!

She called Bottsy and got her. She told what she had found.

"What should I do, Botts?"

"Have you called the police?"

"No, I called *you*."

"For Christ's sake, Quinlan, there's a rapist wandering around loose. Hang up and get the cops."

Elaine did hang up. She sat there a moment, thinking: *No, Bottsy, you're awfully sure of yourself and I never am, but this is no rapist. That much I know. This time I know something you don't know, friend Botts. There's a lot I don't know about this freak, but . . . that cool breath on the skin . . .*

Feeling calmer, Elaine decided to check and see what had been stolen before she called the police. They would ask. Not the record player and amplifier, obviously. She cruised around the apartment. Not her little Sony tube. Not her Masterwork battery radio. Not her strongbox with the junk jewelry. Not her Waring blender. Not her GE Universal can opener. Not a thing. Nothing at all. Not a damn thing.

She dialed the police emergency number.

"Communications center."

"My apartment has been broken into."

SHE thought she heard a siren before she had even hung up. The police began arriving in a minute and a half. Two. Four. Six. Eight. Who do we. . . . They kept coming in partnerships, car by car. Ten. She thought she counted fourteen—but the bluecoats were milling around; maybe there were more, maybe less. It must have been a dull night in old Elm City. Elaine began to blush. Stammer. Justify herself to the taxpayers.

As the clodhoppers trampled her lingerie there were some off-color remarks.

Then one of them said, "It's been jimmied. Look here, lady."

Elaine went to the door. Yes, the wood of the door just

above the latch had indeed been bitten hard. She looked at the doorframe. The wood had scarcely been dented.

She knowingly said, "It's the way they hang these cheap-shit readymade doors."

Several of the cops looked shocked at her profanity.

They said there was nothing they could do. Had to catch 'em in the act.

"You mean even if he's hiding in the cellar?"

"Even he's having a cup of java in your kitchen, ma'am. The Supreme Court would throw it out on its ear. We got to catch him doing it. Don't worry about your cellar. We been over the whole premises. There's nobody anywheres around the place."

"You know," Elaine suddenly popped forth in a loud voice, "I think you guys are a bigger pain in the ass than the freak who made this mess. Why don't you get out of here?"

One of the older policemen, pretending not to have heard her, said in a fatherly voice, "Leave us know if you have any further trouble with this perpetrator, miss."

"Sure," Elaine said, "I'll get a half-Nelson on him next time and hold him till you brothers arrive."

Chapter 11

Affter the police had left and the useless door was shut and she was alone, rocking and rocking in her Cohasset Colonial chair, the fear hit her in a confused rush of out-of-focus mindprints. There was much more than the shape of the freak to reconstruct; much more to deal with than the foggy negatives of her disgust and despair with this elegant-seeming neighborhood. Something was missing in her life. She thought of her childhood friend, Aggie Bent, who had the gift of being bad. Elaine could never achieve more than being Aggie's admiring satellite; she thought of her envy of Aggie, her wish that she could get the knack of being naturally and easily bad. She saw in memory the fuzzy picture of Aggie in the album, wearing a white sailor hat cocked to one side, her face filthy, sluttish, jubilant. Was Aggie's simply the knack of letting go? There was a snapshot in the album of her mother chewing her lip with concentration as she sewed dried leaves—lavender? basil? bayberry? rosemary?—into a lacy bag to put in her lingerie drawer. She remembered Greg saying to her one night, after everything was spoiled between them, "Why can't you get out a belly laugh, El? What a whinny you have!" She was unable to scream. She'd never really had to scream, but without ever having tried, she knew that there just wasn't passageway in her throat for a true shriek. She didn't want to go in her bedroom. She was afraid of the freak's exuberance. She was distressed that nothing had been stolen. Theft would have been so subdued, so culturally determined. She saw herself on her father's knee in the studio photograph on the first page of the album, hair cut straight across in bangs, the little lollipop face with a smirk called up by command of the photographer. There she was. Little Lainie. Now she knew she'd never change. She was Elaine Quinlan. She had been Elaine Quinlan all along. She would be Elaine Quinlan until the day she died. She rocked herself as if she were in a cradle, and wept.

S HE must have sat there tossing in her little boat of memories on her little sea of anxiety for a couple of hours. She thought once of calling Bottsy Feldman and asking if she could come and spend the night, but it seemed to her that Bottsy's way of comforting her would be to engulf her in flesh. She felt smothered by the fantasy of Bottsy's tankard breasts and cask of a belly pressing her own soft sketch of damp clay in against her so breakable armature.

W HEN the doctor, or pseudodoctor, in that green-walled parlor in Asbury Park, New Jersey, its stark white surgical table fitted out with stirrups for a canter on a succubus, had held high in his hand the instrument that looked like the kitchen utensil you use to baste roast fowl, and there within it, sure enough, swam the little worm, or mollusk, or minnow that in its warm wet bed in her belly a few minutes before had been intended to grow up into a man and get into Harvard, to compose at the age of twenty-eight a truly original work founding a new school of phenomenological philosophy, to call up every year on Mother's Day, to play the flute to ease the nerves, to marry the daughter of an incredibly rich manufacturer of unsafe plastic valves for hydraulic auto brakes, and to shoot into that wife from his pleasure gun, after three drinks one cloudy night, millions of tiny polliwogs which would race to find the matrix in the warm wet bed where a new worm, or mollusk, or minnow, might then lodge, intended in its turn to become . . . —and when the doctor said, "That's it, my dear," all she could think to say was, "That was easy."

"Easy as punkin pie," the crooked doc said.

G REG was at the door on his knees fiddling with the lock a flexible key like an angel fish ponytail had come to life lashing flies off his flanks but the stirrups kept coming off her pistol holster was bouncing violently against the blue uniform rocker flew over the landscape of veins on the backs of her mother's hands to push the needle with the thimble on the middle finger ouch mother don't don't *Jesus friend of little children* don't *be a friend to me*

S HE was stiff and her neck hurt. She blinked at the bright light, got up out of the rocker, worked saliva around her dry teeth with her tongue. Memory broke the dam in her sleepy head, and she quickly turned her back on her bedroom. With a jerking swivel she checked the apartment door, that damned door, to make sure it was still shut. Then she took a deep breath, wheeled, walked right in to chaos. This time— perhaps drugged by her dreams—she felt no fear, only a blurry curiosity, then disgust. She kicked the things on the floor into a pile. There among the froufrou was the black lace ultrabikini, with the little red heart appliquéd at The Place, that Greg had bought and made her vamp up and down in, like a topless bimbo in a jack-off bar. "Jiggle your boobs, come on, baby!" Some street scene when he'd bought it!— he'd confessed the whole thing. He was walking along Brattle and suddenly saw himself reflected fullface in the plate glass window of a store—this overeducated bourgeois preppie Ivy Leaguer who had tried to disguise himself as Everyman—and beyond the layer of reflection were these women made of transparent plastic wearing gauzy Krafft-Ebing snatch traps, patriotic rosettes, harnesses of Havelock Ellis ribbon, de Sade leather buttock-straps, tassled pasties, drag panties, G-strings like candle smoke. He looked both ways, then walked right in and bought the little nothing with the heart at the bull's-eye. He tried to pass off the whole caper, including her humiliation, as a piece of social satire. She remembered saying the next day, "I've never known an American man who wasn't both a voyeur and a sadist—except my father, *he* wasn't. You pretend you hate the culture, but you're sewn right into it, Greg. You're just exactly like the man in the gray flannel suit. Exactly."

"Your father!" he'd said. Eye for eye, toot for toot. "That's a laugh. No kinks like Catholic kinks. From what you've told me I bet he was a confession-booth queen."

Then, standing there by the pile of tinted cloth on the bedroom floor, she *forced* herself to think of Greg's gentleness, in the early days, his zany humor, the way he flicked his hand when he made his point, wanting so much for you to agree with him.

Sᴴᴇ changed the sheets. She had just washed them that morning, but the freak's hands had been on them. When she had tucked in a fresh pair she flopped into bed in her jeans and tee shirt. She could not bring herself to undress. Sleep had left her. She brimmed over with Greg-pain. When she had told him she was pregnant—"It must have happened on that lovely beach, Gregsy"—he had blown up in his overcontrolled way. He spoke low, in an even tone. "Can't you even keep track of pills? Christ, El, you know I'm into Z.P.G. I'm *never* going to father a child."

*   *

The company wants you to feel safe. She could hear her
pulse in her ear on the pillow, *shusha shusha shusha.* Those
were not the systole and diastole of a safe person. She kept
hearing *clicks.* Analyzing them. It was amazing the number
of inanimate objects that could eke out *clicks*: drying wood—
kitchen cabinet doors—her alarm clock—could that be static
electricity in that pile of synthetics on the floor? She heard
the door being pried open again and again. Once she started
up into a sitting position out of a half sleep.

Aggie taught her to smoke when they were eight. Aggie
had heard that if you shaved your arms the hair would grow
back like a gorilla's. She swiped her father's Gillette razor
and his Burma Shave brushless cream, and she and Elaine
scraped at their forearms. To Aggie's disappointment their
arms remained human. Aggie's father had had polio, *his* arms
were weak, he had some large polished sea stones that he
used, to keep what little muscle tone he could, with lifting
exercises. Aggie used to hide those stones. When they were
nine, Aggie's mother had a new baby who sometimes turned
blue. Aggie would come running into the room beaming and
would shout, "Hey! Eldridge is turning blue. Let's go watch."
Once she drank a whole bottle of Phillips' Milk of Magnesia
to see what would happen: she did one giant booboo, and
that was that. When they were eleven, she took Elaine into
the confessional with her to hear her lies to the priest.
    Elaine remembered the warning voice of her racing heart
as she crouched down by Aggie's legs to stay out of any possible line of sight of the priest through the listening grille.

*   *

Mᴏɴᴛʜs afterward Greg asked her how she *knew* her father was not a voyeur. What could she say? It was just that her father was the sort of person Greg would never never never be.

Sʜᴇ was walking along a certain sidewalk reaching up to hold her father's hand. "Daddy, don't walk so *fast*."

Sʜᴇ needed to see the snapshot of Greg at Bromley. On skis he was graceful and endlessly seemed to be turning in on himself; his sweep was as hard to believe as that of a Möbius strip. He was clean then, a skeptic; cheerful and generous. She had knitted him a scarf, purple for royalty. He wore it sometimes up over his chin and pretended to be the mysterious author of *The Seven Pillars of Wisdom*; the snow was desert sand. He could set that kind of illusion moving in your mind, until you believed that cold was hot. Elaine turned on the bedside lamp, threw back the covers, doubled and rolled and was up; she skirted the pile and went into the living room and lit a light. Where had she left the album, anyway? She thought it belonged on the plank propped on cinder blocks against the wall beyond the rocker. Not there. She looked in the pile of books. Behind the record player. Where *was* the damn thing? With a new chill around her heart she began to think her past was lost and she was no one at all.

Chapter 12

"O KKIE? You awake?" Macaboy stands at the door to the upstairs apartment.

"Yoost one minute."

Finn Okvent makes deep string sounds out of Sibelius when he speaks. The syllables do their Scandinavian roller-coaster thing, his thick lips kiss the surds and the unvoiced fricatives, and his tongue lolls around liquid consonants and umlauted diphthongs as if they were mouthfuls of baked Alaska. Soon this computer maniac is at the door in his skiv-vies. He has an orange beard and eyes that have come out of sleep somewhat slurry, seeming to contain very thin space matter from the ionosphere.

"Hey, Okkie baby, could you give me a hand this aft?"

"Güve a hand?" Finn looks down at his right hand, which has large freckles on it.

Finn's mental data-base stores something like three trillion bits, capable of being retrieved and delivered to the terminal of his facial expressions at the rate of several hundred bits per second, but his software is deficient: his primary input pro-gram has failed to key in even the commonest American vernacular expressions.

"That means: Help me," Macaboy says.

"Ooh yaw," Finn says, nodding.

"I have to deliver a door. Can we use the camper?"

"Ooh yaw." The nod again. This is a most agreeable Svensker. He hasn't even any coffee in him yet.

"Mind wearing the monkey suit again?"

"Monkey süit?"

"The coverall. You know. Safe-T Securit-E Syst-M."

Okvent laughs. "I am 'Frank' again?"

"You got it, Frankie baby."

THEY are driving, if you can call it that, down George Street. The inventor of the minicomputerized internal combustion engine fuel conservator is at the wheel of the stuttering camper, hanging on like a rodeo cowboy just out of the gate on a Brahma bull with nettles slapped onto his *cojones*. Macaboy is beside him, bracing himself against the dashboard. They are both wearing immaculate company coveralls. *Frank* is written in cursive letters over Okvent's heart.

"She called me early this morning," Macaboy says. "The place had been torn apart. The guy had pried the door open and made himself at home."

"At höme?"

"Walked right in. . . . She accepted the price of the door right off. You'll like her, Okkie. She's got a certain something vague about her that you'd like. This *indefinite* quality. The off look in the eye that so many Irish drinkers have, you know? Aren't Vikings and Celts kissing cousins?"

"But you said you want me to go höme right away?"

"We'll carry the door up—and then there wouldn't be anything else for you to do, old Oks."

They are at a red light at Church Street. The camper is in repose, but it still rattles like a kettle coming to a boil. "Why do you remain in the nineteenth century?" Finn asks. "You are sö intelligent. The universe"—he makes a whole watery song of the word, dipping low under the surface on the first syllable, *yüüniverse*—"is waiting, Macaboy."

"If I had charge of the universe," Macaboy says, "I'd bend the time warp right back on itself. I'd dick around awhile, faster than the speed of light, and then, yes—I might just stop time. Somewhere back there where the basics lived. Wood, stone, wool, cotton, oxygen, wheat, coal, water. Water in a lake so clear you can see the bottom thirty feet down."

Okvent shakes his head with suicidal gloom. "You can't stop it."

"Meanwhile I'll just work with wood, thanks, Okkie."

M ACABOY is amazed how friendly Mzz Quinlan has decided to be.

They have just carried the door up into the hallway outside her apartment.

"Let me see it," she says. She is wearing a thin tee shirt. She has a bra on. She puts her hands on her hips. "Oh, it's a work of *art*," she says. She really seems to mean it. "Did your company actually make this? I'm impressed."

"This is Frank," Macaboy says.

"Hi," she says. "Am I glad to see you guys!"

"Guid day," Okvent says. Macaboy knows this chick has a fast ear, and he fully expects her to ask, with that wood-hasp voice she sometimes uses, if they really christen boy-children Frank in the Land of the Midnight Sun.

But she just says, "A good day after a bad night."

"You insured?" Macaboy asks. "What did they take?"

"That's the scary part," she says. "Not a bloody thing. I can't find my picture album, but I must have stuck it away somewhere. Who'd want that?"

"The place a mess?"

Macaboy sees a ripple go across her face. "No," she says. "Nothing was touched. Oh, yeah," she says, "one of my plant jars got broken. The lights were on. Music going—James Taylor: you think that says anything?"

"Sounds kind of bizarre," Macaboy says. "It's usually your run-of-the-mill druggies looking for a quick hock."

"*That* should really help," she says, nodding at the solid walnut door lying on its long side, propped against the wall.

"Like I said, the company wants you to feel safe." He sees her eyes whip over to his. "And you will," he says, cool.

O KVENT has left. Macaboy digs a spirit level and a flexible tape measure out of his tool box, and after a few passes with the level—his lips are pressed together, he exudes expertise as if it were a natural issue of his working flesh—he explains what he has to do. The casing is slightly skewed. The jambs are almost plumb, but the sill sags on one side and the heading has a swoop in it. He has to cut the door down to fit exactly this slightly crooked doorcase. He has left five-eighths of an inch of overage on each dimension. He will have to do the trimming with planes. The mortise for the lock has already been cut, but he will have to fit a new strike plate and set in new hinges. This is all finicky work. It will take several hours. He may have to work on into the evening. He wouldn't want to leave her overnight with no door. Right?

"I'll fix some supper," she says.

F IRST he removes the old strike plate and cuts tight-fitting plugs for the holes in the jamb and glues them in. These two people are getting acquainted. He thinks: You could slice the caution around here with a butter knife. At their last encounter she came on like an employer—"sonny," "Eddie boy." He put the entire genera of female architects and Bennington women down. She as much as said the day would never come when she would order a new door; he made bright eyes at her when he wobbled the old knob. She has the great advantage over him of having been wrong. There is, besides, a deeper rift—between his tightly calibrated constant turbine energy and her sparky, sputtering, stubborn way of being there and then disappearing, flaring and going dark.

Reasons for dropping out of Reed College. Disillusionment. Vietnam. Ego dilution. Deep-seated toxic reactions. "The Movement seemed like a better education than Sociology 24."

"You must meet my friend Ruth Greenhelge. She's here in New Haven now. She was a real peppercorn in college. You two might have something in common." Implying that "we two" might not?

"What's she doing now?"

"Balling a professor of linguistics. A specialist in logic."

Macaboy's right hand hovers like a helicopter over his next operation. "That was all long ago," he curtly says.

"QUINLAN," he says. "That has to be Irish from way back."

"You use my last name, and I use your first name," she says.

"My name is Macaboy. You'd think that was Irish, too, but it's not, it was French. Maquisbois. They went to Nova Scotia. My mother's side, we're old, old New Englanders—you know, black hats, silver shoe buckles, election—the whole mare's nest."

"Elaine," she says, giving him permission just by saying it.

"You micks tell such incredibly beautiful lies. I mean like Cuchulain, the Fenians, Deirdre, all that. 'Dream-dimmed eyes.' Joyce alone would have been enough. But, Jesus, take those ancient titles. *The Book of the Dun Cow. The Yellow Book of Lecan. The Speckled Book.* It's all there, the whole Irish earthy simplicity bit! Even the *names* of the poets, you can't believe them: Teig Og O'Higgins, Eochy O'Hussey. Hey, have you read Mary Lavin's stories?"

"No, but I've heard of her. I've just been reading Flannery O'Connor."

"You Irish elevate suffering to the level of honor and loyalty and respect for the marriage bond. It's like pain is the highest decency."

He can see the hot specks coming forward out of the sockets. "Life is painful for poor people," she scornfully says. "It takes courage."

"Yeah, I know," he says, mollifying. "I've always wished for that particular kind of courage. But my parents didn't find it convenient to be poor. I gather yours didn't either."

H E sharpens the blade of a long wooden jack plane. He wedges the door, on one side, into a metal bracket he brought along, which holds the wooden leaf upright; he has carefully padded the metal of the brace with old toweling wherever it touches the wood. He has taken measurements in the doorcase a dozen times. He bends to his work. His eyes brim over with the perfection of what he is doing.

She drags her rocker out into the hall and sits to watch him. She does not dare to rock, for fear of causing his eyes to swerve from their strict lines of aim.

He runs a shot of the plane the whole length of the outer side. He bends down and picks up the shaving and holds it high for her to see. It is an exquisite helix, several feet long, and seems alive.

"W HAT did you say her name was—that firecracker from Bennington who's here now?"

"Greenhelge. Ruth Greenhelge."

"I heard her rave once. I was always there at those meetings."

"But I thought you went to Reed. Isn't that in Oregon?"

"I got around."

"I T's true my father wasn't poor," she says. She is still burning from that little reminder of his. "He was a contractor. He worked hard for every cent he earned."

"The well-known Protestant work ethic."

She doesn't laugh. "But the family memory of poverty was always there. Our Quinlans came over in 1832 in a stinking ship's hold with six hundred other immigrants—you know? Cholera broke out on the way over, and when they got to the Narrows, the quarantine people went on board, and they threw every single thing those people owned overboard, just except what they had on their backs, threw away their clothes, bedding, keepsakes—not that they had that much. The Quinlans started over here from *scratch*."

Macaboy is working now on the end grain with a metal block plane. He stands a moment with the plane poised away from the wood. "Yeah," he says, "I read about a thing like that, those immigrants, in *Redburn*. That book made me understand President Kennedy for the first time. I mean, that *drive*."

"I wish I had some of it," she says.

"No," Macaboy says, "you're lucky if you've been spared it."

"**I** worked one summer in a corset factory," he says. "Sorting garments in the company laundry. At the end of the summer, the girls in the office threw a farewell party for me, and they gave me some stuff out of the company line as a going-away present. One thing they gave me—a pink bra with a soupçon of padding in it. We lived in Avon, see, and I knew this girl in East Hartford. It was pretty weird, she was my father's boss's daughter. She had an ass like a Mixmaster, but she could use a little falsification up front. So the night after the farewell party I took the bra to her as a giftie, and while she was unwrapping it she said, like it was something as casual as it's a nice evening, a bit dewy, she says, 'Hey, they fired your old man today.' Some big outfit had taken over the company. Not a word of advance warning. My Pop was about to be fifty. I felt like she'd rapped me in the jewels. So casual.

Like, *Thanks for the falsies, your father's a washout, old buddy.*"

"Would you mind—besides the lock—putting one of those, uh, chains on the door?"

"Not at all. Glad to."

"I'm sorry what I said last time about Bennington chicks all being like Mondrians. That was stupid."

"No. You were perfectly right," she says. "Hard edges. I kind of liked it."

His face is turned away. "You're not," he says. "You're more of a Cézanne."

"Is that supposed to be good?" He can hear a particle of eagerness on the edge of suspicion. "Sounds pretty dull, old hat. It's kitchy. I think I liked the other better."

"There's a haze on the landscape," he says.

"This is a knob lock I'm going to install," he says. "The one advantage is, it opens fast from the inside. I notice this house doesn't have fire escapes—illegal as hell, huh? But with this lock, you can really zip out of here."

"I hadn't even noticed about the fire escapes."

"I was surprised you knew so much about Wooster Square."

"Oh, that's just company policy."

"I adore this square. Mixtures make the strongest unities. I was in Venice once"—he nods, almost as if he has heard her say this before—"when my father gave me this trip as a graduation present. And Piazza San Marco—I don't mean to say Wooster Square is *that* good—but the mixture is what makes them both, you know? The church itself, then the Cam-

panile, the Library, the Loggia, the Moors' clock tower—
those funny figures hammering out the hours."

"Yeah," Macaboy says, "and St. Theodore stepping on a
crocodile."

"What do you mean? Where is that?"

"On top of one of those two columns. You know, in the
approach—the Piazzetta."

"Mr. Macaboy, you are one weird locksmith."

"I don't know about that," he says, ocular energy pouring
along a ruler's-edge line toward her, "but one thing I do
know: this door's going to really freak you out, it's going to
be so good."

"What kind of pizza do you like?"

"Anchovies and green peppers. Nothing else."

"Be right back."

Chapter 13

ELAINE tucked her feet up under her on the rocker.
She had the receiver of the phone jammed between her chin
and her left shoulder, and as she talked she inspected her
fingernails as if favorable signs were engraved on them.

"He didn't get finished until after midnight."

"What are you preparing me for?"

"No, nothing like that. He worked straight through,
Greenie, from two in the afternoon till like twelve thirty at
night. With just time out to scarf a pizza."

"He can eat, huh?"

"And with this fierce concentration. I thought the damn
wood would burst into flames."

"You sound pretty hepped up."

"Wasn't a damn thing to get hepped up about. I don't
think he even saw me. Know what he did when he was finished?"

"I'm holding my breath."

"Asked for my vacuum cleaner. Honest to Pete."

"Hey, what are his rates? I could use some of that."

"He talked like something on tape *while* he was concen-
trating. He has this stereo head. He's done the most amazing
reading, Greenie. I mean, for a total dropout. We got onto

my ancestors, and he talked for ten minutes about Irish labor laying the railroad tracks here in the East—the routes, where the lumber for the ties came from, the mills that made the rails, he had it all down."

"What about the door?"

"Oh, Greenie, you should see it. The grain is—I don't know—like taffeta."

"Come again?"

"It's natural color. He rubbed on some stuff, Skandia Oil, two coats—applications, I guess you'd call them. It just glows. He left the oil for me to put more on."

"Sounds like the old backrub routine."

"You should hear the sound it makes when it clunks shut. . . . Oh, hey, by the way. He said he'd heard you make a speech once at some rally."

"Oh? What did he say?"

"Nothing, really. He just picked up on your name."

"My name? How did that come up?"

"I don't know—he was talking about his political phase, and I said you'd been very into all that at Bennington, he ought to meet you. That was all."

"What's his name?"

"Macaboy. Eddie Macaboy."

"Never heard of him."

Hᴇʀ back itched. She flicked on her little Sony tube. Out of the crackling snow came Harry Reasoner, looking her right in the fizz. He seemed to be trying to comfort her. And yet. Our bombs were guided by laser beams so they would hit the power plant but not the dam three hundred feet away. The cloudburst dumped on the Black Hills and crested in Rapid City—hundreds of autos, flushed out of town, were strewn over the railroad tracks. Body count at Anloc: 114. A curly-haired blond youth walked out of the ocean at Key West, in cutoff jeans and a tee shirt, with a rusty knife on his belt and a cheap compass in his pocket; he couldn't remember his name, his family, where he was from, how he got where he was, wherever that was. "It's like"—he was frowning, the effort showed—"it's like a wall in my mind." There was a place between her shoulder blades that Elaine could not reach to scratch.

SHE sat looking at the door and feeling its reproach. The very precision of the carpentry seemed a reminder of her vagueness. She felt like thumbing her nose at the damn door. She was a useless person. Her days rubbed her raw. She felt that she was decent, she honored her promises, she was sensitive to others' feelings. Lot of good any of that did. An image of her hardworking, gentle father crossed her mind. He was leaning down over her, saying, "Nice going, Lainie." His praise was like a warm bath. Personnel directors humiliated her; she was sick of being told that her education had aimed too high. She had tried everything but Yale. No one wanted her. It was hard for her to get moving. Mornings were difficult. How could she possibly have thrown away two years on a man who was disintegrating? The walnut was well cured, Macaboy had said, it was just about warp-proof, but it might swell in a long stretch of wet weather, in which case he'd gladly come and plane down any sticking places. Those manic goo-goo eyes! She never wanted to see him again. She didn't want to be a bluish hill in an Impressionist painting. To face the fact, she had never felt so unsafe in all her life.

Chapter 14

M ACABOY, at the lockeyist bench, cutting some keys
for a cylinder job on Bradley Street, is hit by a downward
pull in his gut that has to do with his father. His mother's
letter is on the television set. Macaboy thinks of all the years
when he was so snotty to both parents. His father always
maintained a correct stance, always said: I love you   if you
need money   we're crazy about your girl   it's up to
you   keep in touch   your mother sends love with mine
. . . all those proper formal mouthings that drove Macaboy up
the wall and across the ceiling. *You don't feel anything! It's
all out of some horrible manual.* But the years went bang
bang bang and then one time—he remembers exactly when it
was, he was visiting Stanford, getting ready for a demonstration against some Dow Chemical recruiters which was going
to involve red oil paint on stone, *very* hard to remove—when
out of the blue he felt as if he had received a weak, weak
signal, like one of those radio impulses the astronomers pick
up that hint of intelligent life on a distant planet: it was
some kind of psychic telegraphy from the old man which took
the form of a spasm of self-doubt. But he did nothing about
it. He sloshed the red paint on the granite wall. Bang bang
bang more years. Then, just a month or so ago—*before* this
letter, thank God—he was going through some old junk and

came across a picture of his father in college, and he shuddered. The cold wind of time bit him. He had a foretaste of mourning. He sensed a coming year when he would no longer look anything like his own Reed pictures. He made a move adulterated by both pity and self-pity. He called up. He apologized for all the shit. *I admire you and I'm sorry.* He knew he had been bound to make the move. He felt so lucky to have made it before his mother's letter came.

"Hello."

"Is this Mzz Ruth Greenhelge?"

"Speaking."

"I'm calling for Safe-T Securit-E Syst-M, Incorporated. My company has instructed me to ask you a few—"

"Knock it off, Macaboy."

"Shiver my timbers, how did you know my name?"

"You're aware of a certain Quinlan?"

"Oh, her. We can't sell you a new door, then? How about a rim lock?"

"She says that's a classy door your company made for her."

"Yeah, we do prime work."

"She also said you said you'd heard me speak."

"Yeah, I was back East, I think it was 'sixty-eight—I think it was just before the New Hampshire primary, like in Hanover? That be possible?"

"Yes. In praise of Gene McCarthy. Does that sound a bit kookie now?"

"That was a bad spring." Lyndon Johnson withdrawing— that really hurt the Movement. Then McCarthy pooping out, hating kids. Martin Luther King in April. Bobby Kennedy in June. Chicago. "We all started going haywire after that."

"Haywire? Speak for yourself."

"Like to talk about it sometime?"

"Not specially. Well. Yes. Yes, I would."

*   *

THIS bushy-tailed Macaboy dibble-dabbles his index finger in the doorbell as if it were the bellybutton of Miss Happiness herself.

In time a tall woman answers. One look at the dangerous expanse of off-white enamel uncovered by what must surely have been intended as a polite smile, and the edge is off Macaboy's speculations. Is his face a billboard of disappointment? If it is, she seems not to read it. "Be right with you," she says, and whirls off to get a purse. Back at the door she opens the bag in his presence and drops a ring of keys into it, jingling them at him first as if she thinks he's kinky for keys. Is this flibbertigibbet in a shortish skirt and a cardigan sweater the great Greenhelge of the fell tongue?

They walk to the Old Heidelberg at a good clip. They get a table nubbled with carved initials in a booth in the bar. Sipping vodka like any pair of middle-class swinging singles, they chat about The Revolution That Wasn't.

At first the memories pour out helter-skelter. It's like a flirtation of two newly-mets, in which memories of songs both knew before they knew each other set up harmonic vibrations in present time. The mere naming of names is enough to empower the poles of a magnetic field. Kewadin. Carl Oglesby. PLP. Jeff Shero. Stokeley. Clear Lake. Carl Davidson. Greg Calvert. T-O Institutes. Vietnam Summer. Huey. Peace and Freedom Party. The Berrigans. Pentagon. Tet. Bernadine. Lexington. East Lansing. Fred Gordon. Spiro Agnew. *New Left Notes.* RYM. Hayakawa. Venceremos. Weather. Kick-ass tactics. Panthers. The Cleveland mindfuck. The Four Days.

"You didn't need a rectal thermometer to know who the assholes were," he says.

Her back is up. Her fingers tremble at the lip of her glass. They disagree about some of the names. Tom Hayden. Mark

Rudd. They quarrel. Old acrimonies, which have been lying like sediment in them, are stirred up. They cannot find the handles of facts; there is a kind of inner swirling that comes from recalling rage—rage which fed on itself as it missed its targets again and again and simply splattered up against the wall. In the years since those tantrum days each has reached a certain level of stability—yet here they are apart, too: she, tending toward convention; he . . . where is he going? he wonders. Filing the burr off new-cut keys, planing and sanding, calibrating, staking his entire worth on fitting things together as tightly as the yin fits the yang. He is suddenly angry at what makes him happiest—perfect joining. Then his anger veers toward big-tooth, here, this woman who still has muted access to her sarcasm of those old ranting days and can still slash.

"Know why I came to Hanover to hear you that time?" he says. "I wanted to see your famous legs. Guys everywhere told me you had the greatest gams east of the gasworks."

"Come off it." God, she's pleased. She moves her thighs under the table on the seat in the booth.

He is drawn further. "I hear you're taking a course in logic between them nowadays."

That gets to the mark. "Your friend Quinlan," she spits out.

And with that, Macaboy realizes his real reason for having wanted to talk with Ruth Greenhelge. "She didn't mean any harm," he says. "She was just talking about how we've all changed." He dills her down, stroking her softly, softly, like a finished door panel with linseed oil and OO steel wool. And in time he can ask, "What was your pal Quinlan like at Bennington?"

"THERE was a period in junior year," Greenhelge says, "when she wasn't making connections. She was worried about it. She said she'd know she was in a room with a person, but

there was a plate of glass between her and the person. Words
could go through the glass, looks could go through it, but
temperament couldn't penetrate it. 'The real *you* bounces off
it,' she'd say. In that very period, she was at her warmest, she
seemed to be right *there*, I really loved her then. I guess she
was desperate, trying to get to you through the glass. She was
a bit spacey, but at the same time she was witty as all get-out,
her mind was working at wild speed. She was a top student in
Russian, and she could talk this imitation Russian at a great
rate—you know, macaronic, mixing in English and French
and Spanish words but all with Russian endings and pronun-
ciations, and if your mind could go with her fast enough, it
all made some kind of out-of-bounds sense."

"She had this funny thing of only being able to speak to
one person at a time. There'd be three of us talking, let's say
Quinnie and me and this Bottsy Feldman, and Quinnie
would aim everything at me. If she wanted then to get something over to Botts, she'd look at me and say, 'Tell her so-and-
so'—with 'her' right there in front of her. It was as if she were
some kind of radio and could only transmit on one frequency
at a time."

"Yes, she had a boyfriend at Dartmouth—to me he was a
bad influence. He was a weirdo—half jock, half weenie.
Amazing dexterity—he took up tossing Indian clubs, and like
one year he got to the International Jugglers' Association
world championships. That was before he went pill-happy.
He was quite funny, but his humor was mostly putdowns. A
lot of it was directed at Quinnie. She sat there taking it. She
could dish it out, too, but she was never cruel like he was."

*　　*

"I COULD never get her going in the Movement. She has a stiff back, that girl. She *cared* about things, but she saw through motives. She saw through me. I've never told anybody this, Macaboy, but I felt *ashamed* when I talked with Quinnie. She knew all about power without ever seeming to need it."

Chapter 15

GREENHELGE on the pipes. She seemed to Elaine to be talking down to her from a great height. Many topics: How was the door? Any luck job-hunting? Status of her own research. The logician in a cranky mood. Sounds, through all the chatter, of exultation. Elaine began to feel the old telephone-tightness in her throat.

"Your friend Macaboy took me to dinner last night. God, is he a charmer! We went all back over the Movement. Actually, we discovered we were at the same protest rally together once without knowing it, the time Rusk spoke to the Foreign Policy Association at the New York Hilton, the first trashing either of us was in on. Neither of us knew it was going to happen. They were throwing bottles and bags of cow's blood and paint and garbage at the cops and the limousines that pulled up. Macaboy said it turned him off trashing for good. We went to the Heidelberg. He is so *bright*."

Elaine was damned if she was going to ask any questions. Greenhelge's voice, from up there, just begged for questions. *Did he talk about me at all? Did he ask about me? Where'd you go after dinner? What did you do, did you . . . ?*

*   *

Snarl of the foyer buzzer. She talked into the intercom grille on the kitchen wall: a pattern of perforations in a round plate, some of the holes half blocked with wrinkled driblets of ancient paint. Speaking into that hideous metal ear she felt disembodied; the abstract Force of Interrogation stood in for Elaine Quinlan. "Who is it?" After stirring a few tendrils of lint in the holes, the sounds seemed to go dead beyond the wall plate.

But at once a tinny vibration came back at her from the grille. "It's the Fuller Brush man." A gargling robot standing in for Macaboy the locksmith and laughing boy.

Reflex: She pressed the release button before she remembered Greenie's call.

The knock came soon.

She opened the door only a crack—she kept it on the chain. In the gap she could see Macaboy's steeply tilted head, cut off aslant at forehead and chin by jamb and door stile. She had a weird moment of slicing his skull along those planes: miracles!—the upper geometric section showing the almost woodlike dense channels and flat nucleated disks of the carapace, and within it, the intricately folded sac of gray and white evasions and betrayals; and the lower section, even more beautiful—a marbleized design of bone and dentine and enamel and mucous membrane and fibrous root of tongue where deceit would be embedded. . . .

"I came by to see if you're feeling—"

"Go away," she said, "you creep."

He had a plant in a jar for her. "The woman said it's a pothos. Check out the Greeks on that word. That's why I picked it." He showed it to her in the crack. Leaves streaked with lemon yellow. He could not pass the jar through with the door on the chain. He urged her, again and again, to open up, but she kept telling him to go away.

"If I'm such a creep, why do you stand there talking to me? Why don't you slam the door in my face? Is it because you know I wouldn't have any trouble getting in if I really wanted to?" The chain, he pointed out, was a psychological deterrent to entry, not a physical one. All he would have to do would be to put his shoulder into it and . . .

"Go away!"

He put the terrarium down on the floor just outside the door and left.

Chapter 16

MACABOY is puzzled. His day is crowded yet empty. He has three jobs. He charges up and down the streets of New Haven on his bike with a sense that the chain is slipping on the sprocket: he seems to be getting nowhere. He is not whistling. A lady, fishing in her crammed pocketbook for change, put her home key ring down on the checkout counter at the York Street Pegnataro's and left it there; it was gone when she went back for it; she is convinced a housebreaker picked it up; she wants a new set of cylinders. Macaboy is not used to finding people boring; he has always said that monomanias were fascinating. Hers is not. The welfare system. She runs it ragged. Freeloading breeds crime. He is so ear-weary when he finishes that he charges her fifteen dollars instead of the usual twelve for a key change—a three-dollar lip tax. When he gets back to Lynwood Place he starts his monthly inventory of key blanks. The phone rings. Safe-T Securit-E Syst-M is listed in the Yellow Pages. A woman on Fountain Street. Her son called her yesterday to say that he had broken his wife's arm in an argument, and the mother had been so upset that when she came in from shopping she left the key in the front-door lock. All night. It was there in the morning, but she was afraid some half-breed criminal had taken it and had it copied and then come back and put it in the lock again to make her unwary. Yes, she actually used the phrase "half-breed." Macaboy never argues with a client. Out the door. On the bike. This woman weeps for her son's unhappiness while Macaboy works. He is distressed that he has nothing to say except that she should be glad it wasn't the other way around, her *son* with compound fracture of ulna and radius. Lots of women nowadays, he says, can break both the bones in a man's forearm. Has she heard about the Equal Rights Amendment? It applies, he says, to the right to break bones. Women have that right. Home again. He completes the inventory. Makes himself a baloney, salami, tomato, and sauerkraut submarine. The mail comes. Two of his checks have bounced. Locksmithing doesn't quite pay. But it is not that he is short of cash. He has income from a trust fund, set up by his father when Macaboy went into the Movement, to prevent—as his father put it—"the fruits of my life's work going to a bunch of God damn red Wobbly anarchist hippies"; the trust fund made Macaboy's employment a condition of its dole. No work, no get. Macaboy is not supporting himself; worse, he can't bother to enter the amounts of checks on the stubs. Is this a way of life for a philosopher? The phone rings. It is a Yale art student with a likely story. He gave a key to his loft to a model. He has finished painting her. He does not need to have her sit for him any more. He therefore wants a key change. Out the door. On the bike. The loft is on Grand Street. While Macaboy is slipping out the old cylinder the artist offers to show him a painting of the key-carrying model. Macaboy is not even in the mood to see a nude at two p.m., but he never argues with a client. The artist drags out a canvas. The style is Abstract Expressionless. There is a muddy red splotch on a greenish-grayish marbleized field. "You really needed a key change," Macaboy says.

Where is the fun Macaboy usually gets from life? He drops in to see Okvent when he gets home.

"Okkie," he says. "Remember that door we delivered the other day?"

"Ooh yaw."

"It has led to nothing but trouble."

Chapter 17

SHE thought that if she turned over, shifted, dug into enough chattels, she might find her lost past: the album. As she searched she remembered snapshots of herself in it: aged nine, on Halloween, with Aggie Bent, both dressed as witches—Aggie looking like one of the ten Salem girls standing before the judges, sexfiend-eyed, possessed, speaking in tongues; while Elaine looks like an adorable trick-or-treat cutie dressed up to attract Tootsie Rolls and Good and Plentys. She wondered, digging in her closet, why she wanted to recover this past of hers at all. Aged thirteen, trying hard to please her father, as she imagines, by being a tomboy, holding up a limp catfish she has caught in the algae-green pond out beyond the Ace Laundry—her wrist bent as if by an intolerable weight, her face straining to cap the horror she feels at this mutated throwback's whiskers and fat-man's mouth. Aged fifteen, dressed for her first dance, in a confectioner's dream of ribbons and pleats and furbelows, and *wearing Mary Janes.* She fell to her knees on the closet floor. She blamed her mother. What fairy tale was her mother trying to push her toward? And why did she let herself be pushed for so long?

*   *

She rose and quickly walked to the row of not yet un-packed storage boxes along the back wall of the living room. She routed frantically in them. She hauled out the Bell hand grain grinder and threw it with a crash in the middle of the floor. She burrowed again and came up with her broken Clairol hair drier and threw it, *clatter*, beside the grinder. She went into the kitchen and got her spun-steel wok, which she hadn't used for two years, and carried it back, and *bong*. From the box, her McAlister bean sprouter. Her Fleming bottle cutter, with which, for a month way back in Greg time, she made hideous glasses from Pepsi and 7-Up bottles. Her Indonesian incense brazier, long empty of sand. At last, at *last*, she was going to shed the dregs and lees of Greg and of . . . and of . . .

She looked at her dulcimer. How many hours and hours had she sat over that melancholy little box, picking out "The Dew Is His Pearls" and "Sit Ye Doon My Faily-Foot" and "Aysters and Crayfish Me Hearties"? She moved toward it, faltered. She wanted both to keep it and to smash it into a thousand splinters in the shapes of quavers and clefs and rest marks and sharp signs and all reminders of all that practice that made imperfect. Somehow she could not part with it—yet.

There was a knocking. From somewhere under her. Oh, God, the Plentaggers. She could just see the poisoner stand-ing on a chair and poking at the ceiling with a broom handle to protest against the noise she had been making.

She ran into the bedroom and wrenched open one of the drawers in which she kept her underclothes. She weeded out the old relics first—the nylons and rayons—and dropped them in a pile on the floor. She had some slips that she would *never* wear—out they came. Greg's black bikini panties with the red heart—onto the throwaway pile. She held up a borderline nightgown that she hadn't worn for a long time, trying to decide . . .

"Looks like the proverbial sheeit hit the proverbial fayan."

A male voice. Right behind her.

In a reflex of terror her hands rose, perhaps to protect her face; the nightgown flew up flaglike. She turned, holding the fabric high, as if she were hiding nakedness.

A strange man was standing in the doorway to her bedroom, grinning.

SHE had not recognized him at first, because he was not in his Safe-T Securit-E Syst-M coveralls but in jeans and a blue work shirt.

"Oh, it's *you*," she said, enormously relieved. Then, with realization, more sharply: "How'd you get in here?"

He reached in the breast pocket of the work shirt and pulled out two delicate tools of a sort she had never seen. "I picked the lock," he said. "Those Framingham knob locks— easy to get into as a bitch in heat." He put the rake and pressure wrench back.

"My chain!"

"I told you last time, those chains just psych people out. They're nothing, nothing." This time a hand went into a rear pocket of his jeans and came out with a compact, rugged hand wire cutter. "Don't worry," he said, the other hand going into still another pocket, "I brought an extra," and he pulled out a spare chain with its doorcase plate. "I'll put it on for you."

"You're just a fucking crook, aren't you?"

"Hey, the line between legit and illegit is very fine, in this world. Look. I'm good at what I do. I don't have to take a key into my shop to copy it. I only need to have it in my hands for three seconds. See, what I do, I press it hard on the inside of my left wrist, and that makes a print of the cuts in the key.

It stays there an amazing length of time. Try it sometime. I can mosey back to the shop, figure the code from my wrist, and cut a blank. Then I have your key. I've developed these skills. You say I'm a crook. I say I'm a craftsman. I admit that covers some ground, if you think of the meanings of the word 'craft.' Huh?"

"You have one hell of a nerve breaking and entering on a woman at eleven o'clock at night."

"Thing is, I have a present for you," he said. "Last time you made it extremely difficult for me to deliver a *cadeau*. This one's bigger than the other was. I wanted to make sure it got into the premises."

She half-turned and dropped the nightgown on the pile of castoffs. Looking away from him she said, "Thank you for the what did you call it? The plant? I've never seen one just like that. What did you mean, about the Greeks?"

"Pothos—he's this young guy with wings. Look up what he's interested in. Why should I tell you?" She kicked at the heap on the floor, rounding it up. "Know something, that plant would have got me in here real easy last time," he said, "without me even breaking the chain. All I had to do was talk to you through the crack, with the chain on, see, the way we did, then when you say, 'Go away,' I put the plant down, like I did, and then pretend to leave. But I wait a few seconds and tiptoe back and hide beside the door. Pretty soon curiosity gets the best of you and you take the chain off and open the door and reach down for the little glass jar, and THEN!" Macaboy raised his hands with the fingers curved into grizzly-bear claws and he let out a two-ton growl. Elaine staggered backward and got her feet caught in her scrap heap and almost fell.

"Damn you," she said.

"Aren't you interested in your present?"

"Look, I'm trying to get *rid* of stuff."

"That's not very nice. When a gentleman—"

"That lousy door you sold me, with all that talk about the

satin texture of walnut—it's not worth—not worth cheese, is it?"

"I could give you a better lock." His face has cheerfulness dabbed all over it as if written in icing on a birthday cake.

"You said I'd be safe as a church."

"The Stanloc people have come out with one that has cuts on the keys that are beveled at different angles—you just cannot copy the keys. Mean bugger to pick, too. I would definitely recommend a Stanloc."

H E sat on a fat DR cushion on the floor, she was in her rocker. His present was between them—a dwarf orange tree.

"My mom used to make marmalade from the little oranges on one of those," he said. "After it bears, you want to cut it way back and let it rest several weeks. Then you start feeding it again—acid plant food."

"My mother couldn't stand cooking."

"Mom would put up tomatoes, watermelon pickles. The great thing was mince pie at Thanksgiving, I used to help dice the suet, all that. When she deep-fried doughnuts, she'd cook the holes for me."

"We ate in restaurants three-quarters of the time. Or frozen TV dinners."

Elaine felt that their sentences were flying past each other, never meeting in the space between them. She knew that when strangers are trying to find each other, the talk goes round sooner or later to mothers, but here, talking to this Eddie person, the essential surrender in that kind of talk—the willingness, or even the urge, to let down defenses and become childlike—was lacking. It was a matter of trust. How could she trust anyone who kept grinding out such flawless cheeriness? The only people she'd encountered who had Macaboy's sort of impervious, unshakable good nature were Jesus freaks. It was true that his smiles didn't seem as automated as theirs always did; he seemed to smile because he felt good. Perhaps the trouble was that she couldn't associate that good feeling, if it was indeed real, with herself. It was something separate; he was in a bottle of his own joy. Sometimes Greg had seemed this way, transiently, on chemicals. Macaboy was not druggy; the pupils of his eyes were as clear as a polar wind. What was he on?

"Look, begin at the beginning, would you?"

"Beginning? What beginning?"

"Of you."

"What do you mean?"

"I mean tell me. Start at the beginning."

HE leaned back on his hands. "I was born Theodore Edmund Macaboy in Avon, Connecticut, on September twenty-third—"

"Hey! Would you mind saying that name again?"

"It's the only name I have, I don't like to wear it out. O.K., Theodore Edmund Macaboy."

"Oh, man. I thought that's what you said. Oh, man. What a con artist!"

"How's that?"

"T. E. M.?"

"My initials. So?"

" 'Our company wants you to feel safe.' Oh, brother."

"Huh?"

"Yeah, your initials. Exactly. There's no company, is there? Safe-T Securit-E Syst-M.—T. E. M. It's just *you*, isn't it?"

Macaboy burst out laughing. "There *is* a company. I'm incorporated under the laws of the State of Connecticut, sometimes called the Land of Steady Habits."

"But what about that other guy? In the company outfit? That Swede you said was named Frank?"

"You don't miss a trick, do you?"

"Oh, Jesus H. Croust, I've been missing plenty tricks. Oooh. 'We'll send this young fellow named Eddie. Handsome type. Ponytail.' "

Macaboy was loving this, showing a lot of teeth. "The dispatcher didn't lie to you, did he? He was a good-looker, wasn't he?"

"What about the Swede? Do you have other guys working for you?"

"No, he's a mad computer genius. It's just a uniform, for when I need help, like delivering a door. I get someone like . . . like Frank to help me, and he wears the monkey suit."

"Then *you* made it? Yourself?"

"The door? Sure."

"It's so beautiful. I sit here staring at it."

Chapter 18

Once there was a windstorm. They were still living in Avon. It was a baby twister, in May, when ill-met frigid and torrid airs of a late New England spring did a dance together down off the traprock ridge and uprooted six fifty-foot Austrian pines that were his father's favorites. His father decided to try to right them and keep them alive. He rigged a block and tackle to the big oak and put two neighbor men and little Eddie and his weak older brother Arden on the fall of the tackle with him. The memory of his father's gritted teeth stays with Macaboy to this day. The lips pulled back. Great pain of trying. The effort of the Elect. Hideous joy of physical labor. Love of the trees and rage at the God of funnel winds. Teeth that could bite! Power in the huge arms and in the jaws. He dreams those teeth sometimes.

On the platform at the railroad station the family was seeing Arden off, when Arden went away to Loomis for the first time. Before the train pulled in Arden put a paper clip on the track. The conductor lifted Arden up, as if he were no heavier than a chicken, onto the metal steps of the railroad car. Then Arden in his ridiculous huge fur hat waved out the train window to them. Runnels of water shone down on either side of his enormous nose. The tears made Eddie feel ashamed. Then the train pulled out and all that was left was the print of the clip on the steel of the rail.

EDDIE begged to go and watch his father play basketball at the Grange. "Not on your life. A school night, son." He was in first grade. He resorted to a strategy of shuttling back and forth between his mother and father. Toward some exceptional requests she was more lenient, toward others, he. Sometimes Eddie was forced to make one parent feel more cruel than the other for a time, then to reverse the pressure. This cross-whipping usually worked. At last he heard his mother say to his father, "One late night wouldn't be the end of the world, would it?" A mild answer: "Whatever you think." Getting his way was so often an anticlimax. And so he went. Father's face, as his Keds heavily slapped the shiny boards with their painted circles and keys and zones of magic, wore a haggard, lost, and pleading look, and his eyes were puzzled and liquid with what seemed to be a fear of murder, his wrists flapped, his fingers were like grasshopper legs, and his random hands were unable to grasp the bouncing sphere, which seemed alive and angry and energetic, and always got away. Why, he looked like Arden! Father! Father! Afterward, Eddie was drawn by a kind of suction into the locker room, and he grew light-headed in the stink of dark armpits and rubbery wet socks, and then he was suddenly melted down in his own sweat to nothing but a pair of eyes staring at these huge beasts ripping off jock straps until he was nearly blinded by what had always, until then, been denied in the Macaboy household: nakedness. He was totally unprepared for what he saw at the base of each broad and web-printed belly: a wig of unnaturally tangled hair, out of which hung a great, limp, yellowy, bodiless turtle neck and head. That would not have been so bad in itself, because he himself

owned a little unwigged model of such a thing, but behind
and below each of these he saw swinging like a nanny goat's
huge milk sac a great dependent wrinkled bag containing two
olives—no, bigger, bigger—two plums, two loaves, two foot-
balls, two blimps. These monstrosities swayed and slapped as
the deep-voiced statues strode glistening to the showers. He
could not tell which was his father. Eddie breathed steam,
and his heart pounded with the wildest joy he had ever
known.

H E sees a croquet court laid out on the lawn in the shade
of the massive poplars his grandfather planted along the
driveway after the old boy had taken a trip to France and had
been stunned by all the leagues of pollarded *allées* there.
Arden stooped over his mallet, awkward and cross. His poor
shot deflected off a wicket, and his blue-striped ball ran to
within two feet of Eddie's yellow-striped one. Taking his
time, Eddie easily tagged Arden's. Then Eddie nestled his
ball against Arden's and held his own down with his bare left
foot. With a surge of sweet revenge for all the injuries sickly
Arden had done him, he wound up, as if swinging a lumber-
jack's maul. The mallet head whooshed down. He felt a knife-
cut in his instep. The shriek that ripped from his throat was
of pain—but also of delight at seeing Arden's ball fly down
the lawn into the clump of prickly raspberry canes. At once
their mother materialized above him, as he hopped up and
down on one foot. He still remembers what she said then—
not a defense of Arden, not a comfort for his own injury, not,
as so often would have been her way, a citation of a rule, but
a flash of cunning, sharp in her eyes and glacial on her
tongue. "The best tactic, son, in this situation, would have
been—look!—tap the opponent's ball to a place just *beyond*
the wicket he's trying to go through. Then it takes him at
least two shots, maybe three, to get back in position and
through. Do you see?" At that Eddie's foot really began to

hurt. Arden threw down his mallet and stalked away from the game. The picture in Macaboy's mind is of the look of surprise on his mother's face.

"WORK" was the mystery. His father drove off each weekday morning. It was said he was "going to work." In winter the snow tires left their print on the plowed white planes of the driveway: the tracks of the provider making off to hunt for meat. The hunter wore a striped necktie. It was often after dark when the car pushed its cones of light back along the driveway, and his father stamped in from the garage, his chin blue from the day's silent growth of beard. He came home from "work" short of speech. Deep seams like razor cuts ran down on either side of the mouth. There were shadows under the owlbrows.

Chapter 19

SHE rose into the new day in motion, her bed a launching pad. She was not quite sure what had set the g's pushing at her. She felt the thrust. She would get out. She would leave her stuff on the floor. She could part with the damned door. The only questions: How far? Where to land? She walked to the Arrow bus terminal at Whitney and Grove and stood among the waiting passengers, studying schedules. Storrs? Pittsfield? Albany? *Service to All Race Tracks*. Uhn-uhn. No appeal. She went to the Greyhound office on Church Street. There, at the schedule rack, with all dreams of connections anchored in cold print, she could visualize a city on a golden plain, a pall of smoke over steel mills, purple Teton majesties, a north wind chopping Lake Michigan, the whiteness of Telegraph Hill, the sun seen from Mallory Pier at Key West plunging into the sea with a green flash at the very end, dewy spiderwebs early in the morning on a still hedge by a white house in—would it be Avon, Connecticut? No! No! No! No! A woman wanting to buy a ticket jostled her. Elaine flew into a fury at her. "Quit pushing!"

*   *

SHE tried to explain to Bottsy. Bottsy's room was in worse disorder than ever. She was struggling with a draft of the chapter about Pyotr Alekseyevich's second visit to America. There were scraps of this tired Kropotkin all over the floor. Bottsy had put on weight. She was too glad to see Elaine, she hugged until the greeting had begun to turn into something else. Elaine, trying to understand what was happening to herself by explaining it, said the impulse to run away came whenever she felt threatened by repetition in her life. She didn't want to go through the same pattern of moves over and over. Echoes gave her the willies.

"But this guy sounds different from Greg," Bottsy said.

"Something about him when he first spoke to me, he was standing there in the doorway to my bedroom—"

"Not that he sounds all that cool," Bottsy said.

"He'd walked straight through a locked door. With a chain on it."

Bottsy sniffed. "He sounds like kind of a lump to me."

Elaine started to cry. Bottsy took her in her arms. Elaine began to feel the balls of the thick hands rubbing, rubbing, the blunt fingers pressing. "Let go of me," she said, striking out with both elbows. "What is this—a massage parlor?"

THE first time she ran away she was about twelve. Being an only child was like being in solitary confinement. She had clung to cutout paper dolls far too long, just to have other kids around to talk to, to confide in, to laugh with, to challenge, to pick on, and to tear up and throw away when they annoyed her. Endless imaginary conversations, in which she took all parts. She would sit on her bed, with the cutouts arrayed around her. There were usually father and mother dolls, too. The parents fought. One of her paper older sisters, Amy, a prissy, do-goody twerp—different patterns represented

Amy from time to time, but Elaine always used a gray crayon to dot the goop's face with pimples—was always patching up false peace between the father and mother. One time the parents were arguing—dangerously, Elaine realized—about her. The mother wanted to sell her into a dressmaker's sweat-shop; the father threatened to kill the mother with an and-iron. He was holding it over his head, ready to strike. Simpering Amy entered the room, grabbed the andiron from behind just in time, and began to tell the father Elaine's innermost secrets. The father listened with his mouth sprung like a moron's. When Amy had finished her (truthful) recital, the father said, "Elaine is a disgusting toad." Elaine began to sob on the bed. She tore up Amy, ripped the mother to shreds, pulled the father's head off, then stuck it back on with Scotch Tape. Burning with shame, still crying, she jumped off the bed, got a Qantas airline bag her Uncle Pat had given her, packed it with a sweat shirt, a toothbrush, a copy of *Sixth Form at Mallory Towers*, which she was reading just then, and the shiny-throated cutout of her father, and flew down through the house and out the back door. She ran and ran, out toward the town dump. Near dark she climbed in under some chokeberry bushes. It began to drizzle. Her in-dignation thinned out and bled into fear. The misty night air glowed with the orangey nimbus of the town. She crashed out of the bushy tangle and began to run again. Orangutans grasped at her from the murk. At last the joy of asphalt jarred her leg bones. She reached home at about ten o'clock. The reception was delirious, especially her mother's; her father poured himself a bourbon. Her mother's happy tears made her wish she had stayed away longer. Her father dialed the police and, clinking the ice in his glass, told them she'd been found.

S HE went with Greenie to Basel's. Greenhelge knew Macaboy, she would understand. They were seated at a tiny table at the middle of the room. Greenie ordered a kebab. Elaine asked for moussaka, and when it came she found it riddled with eggplant, which had always put hair on her tongue; after the first mouthful she played fork-shove. The zithers were going, and a few real Greek derivatives and some drunken customers were doing a hypnotic dipping-and-hesi-tating dance with linked arms around the tables in a large circle, at the dead center of which was Elaine's heart.

"Look, kid," Greenie said, her pearly choppers making instant lamburger of the kebab, "you're just horny."

"I hate that word."

"People who are getting it don't hate that word. When did you get it last?"

"You crummy slut."

"I *beg* your pardon."

"You slept with him, didn't you?"

"Him?" Greenhelge's long face, growing longer, seemed to Elaine to be stretching innocence to the breaking point. "What him?"

"You know what him. *Him.*"

"Oh, *him!*" She knew, all right. "No, Lainie. You're way off the mark. All he wanted to do was talk about you."

"You're putting me on."

"Think whatever you want."

That was Greenie's way: to leave things hanging out. She couldn't resist giving you a tiny bite for the positive part of your mind to take, then much wherewithal for the negative part to seize and choke on. Elaine began to eat eggplant.

This time she asked Greenhelge to wait in her car until she had had a chance to check her apartment. There was a letter in her mailbox in the entrance hall. She took it out and stuffed it in her purse as she pulled out her keys. Her apartment was locked; dark. She turned on lights and searched. All clear. She ran down and waved to Greenie, who drove off.

Elaine climbed back up, put Carly Simon on the record
player, and sat and rocked, thinking about how her impulse
to flee had died out. It was nearly midnight before she
opened the letter.

It was a printed form, with certain blanks filled in, among
them one for her name, which was misspelled.

Dear *Miss Quinlon*:
Report to work at 9 a.m. the morning after receiving this
notice.
Job classification: *Clerical, Class C.*
Job description: *Filing. Occasional "stenography" in pool for
"junior executive" ranks. Occasional "minuting" of supervisory
staff "straight shooter" motivation stimulation meetings and shop
stewards' "bite the bullet" employe intelligence and demerit meetings.*
Hours: *8:30 a.m. to 4:30 p.m.*
Breaks: *8-minute coffee, 9:30 a.m., 11:00 a.m., 2:30 p.m., 4:00
p.m.; 10-minute "Swedish roll" or "yoghurt", 10:30 a.m.*
All operations punched on time clocks. Tardiness penalized on
paychecks pro rata until "dismissal cut-off," after one hour cumu-
lative delinquence.
Wages: *$3.71 p/hr.*

(Signed) *Maxine Brallery*
Director of Personnel

Elaine went directly to the phone. She heard sounds of Ma
Bell's busy synapses struggling for association, as if the telephone system were a vast failing memory. Seven rings and a
weak hello.

"Hi, Mom!"

"Lainie? Have you any idea what time of night it is?"

"Sorry, Mom. Just wanted to touch base."

"You've waked me up out of that first deep sleep. I'll never
be able—"

"I *said* I was sorry, Mom. I forgot. I never get to bed before
two o'clock."

"This is typical, Lainie, typical. There's just a total lack of consideration for others."

"I wanted to tell you I have a job."

"You have never tried to put yourself in another person's position. Your father and I—what kind of a job?"

"I'm manufacturing hand guns."

"You're what?"

"Saturday night specials."

"Darling, are you on some . . . some medication?"

"It's an outfit called the Lampson Gunsmithy. Big. I'm really not making the guns. I just make Xerox copies of clichés in quotation marks and stick them in metal drawers."

"How long have you been working?"

"Three weeks."

"Lainie! Shame on you! I can hear one of your little white lies four hundred miles away. I've always been able to tell when you were fibbing."

"O.K., Mom. I start tomorrow."

"Do you have a boyfriend?"

"Yep."

"Oh, dear. Is he nice?"

"Of course."

"Does he shave?"

"*Yes*, Mom. He wears a ponytail, though."

"Oh, dear, Lainie, don't make a mistake. Promise me one thing—you won't get married without bringing him out to meet your mother."

"*Married?* Who's getting married? . . . You'd like him, Mom. He's so . . . so exact."

"What does he do?"

"He's a locksmith. And a carpenter. You should see the door he made for me."

"The what?"

"Door. Door! *Door!* Can you hear me?"

Sounds of weeping.

"Oh, Mom, for Christ's sake."

"On top of everything else you take His name in vain."

"I'm *sorry*, Mom. I just wanted to fill you in."

"Sometimes I can't believe you're Thomas Quinlan's daughter."

"Oh, shit, Mom, don't start that. . . . I *love* you."

"I wish I could believe that." *Click*.

Chapter 20

THE heat was like a hawk. It soared with glittering parental eyes, looking for her; it saw her; it hovered directly over her, close-shouldered, slowly flapping its wings to stay in one place, poised to dive and kill. The image of a hawk came often to Elaine. She could not remember whether the bird had been set in motion in back of her eyes by a memory, or a dream, or something she had read as a child. It filled her with anxiety; or perhaps anxiety blowing through her started it wheeling. It was over her in heat that evening, as she walked out Chapel toward home after her first day at work.

Her head had been spinning all day—the hawk in high spirals—with something like the dizzy muddle she felt whenever she came back to familiar rooms after a long time away. (Stale air. Mail to be opened. Dust. Memories. Brown water from faucets. Motes of the past hanging in the air.) The office of the factory was a huge overlighted space of acrylic partitions and insect sounds. There was no sense at all of explicit manufacture. The company might have been in the business of fabricating amicus curiae briefs or petcocks for sump pumps, for all you could tell by the lazy, indifferent girls, mostly in very short skirts, whispering, flapping papers like signal pennants, eyes out for the bitch supervisor. No sense at all of guns but a great deal of killing. Of time. No one seemed to work at all. There was a high cunning in the gold-bricking all around Elaine. The flirtation with idleness was almost like a game of sex. She felt quite stupid, doing what she had been told to do. The filing took no brains; she yearned for more stupidity than she would ever have. Invoices by date and number. The girls were not curious about her. They looked at her, she thought, reproachfully. She felt marked, like Hester Prynne, as if she had a shameful varsity letter embroidered on her breast. In fact a college education might be far worse than adultery with some of these chicks. The windows were sealed; the air was chilly; the dead, egg-crated light made people's eyes look like caterpillars. What kind of sadomasochistic apparatus had she wandered into? Why? In order to be able to tell her mother she had a respectable job? So as not to go dum-dum, rocking and staring at that ferking walnut door?

Late sunlight leaned in to her side of the street. She was sopping. How could she face a job in summer in an air-conditioned office?—going home was going straight to hell. She skidded past the pizza parlors, her gorge tightening at the mere thought of molten cheese. She had some raspberry sherbet in the freezer compartment of her fridge; she would try that, and some iced tea. Yes. She stopped at Cavaliere's and bought a crisp, dewy bunch of mint out of the cold case. Starting up Academy Street she held the mint to her nose to sniff the coolth of some brookside copse she wanted to imagine, but the hairy leaves tickled her nostrils and made her sneeze.

Something reminded her of something. . . . A vague stimulus—eyes?—ears?—seemed to be trying to break through her confusion. There! Up ahead. That round-shouldered lope, leaning forward into the pace. Less than half a block up Academy. It was, without a doubt, the melancholy slant of Homer Plentagger. A man at the door of her memory, half draped, as if in used towels, in that huge terrycloth robe. She slowed her steps. She hoped he would not look back and see her. She thought of ducking across the street into the park, but she could tell that the shadowy murk trapped under the oaks and sycamores was simply heat so still as to have been condensed into darkness. She walked with care.

The poisoner was almost at the house. He would look in all his pockets for his keys, fumble in his letter box; clocks everywhere would stop their ticking over the time he would take. She was on the point of turning about face, to get away from something evitable in this world, when—

What? What was flipping up there? A fast blur from the mouth of Court Street, beyond. Then dark bees zigging around the pesticides man, some kind of dancing ritual. She made out three shapes dodging around the tall, mournful figure. His arms began to cut the air decisively, as if he were a speeded-up home-plate umpire.

Elaine, still walking, sweating, realized she was getting close to something she did not understand, did not want to understand. Sometimes she went to a movie rated R, in which it would turn out that the rating was to protect children of tender age from sights adults were presumed to take as matters of course. A blood-sopped horse's head in a gangster's bed. A writer rendered vegetable by a gang of clockwork nasties. She had learned to close her eyes fast. She did that now. She could not walk with her eyes closed. Before her whirling neurons could scramble together a halt, she looked to see where she was going.

Instead she saw three men running at her. They were wearing multicolored ski masks, the eye circlets like bathysphere portholes. Elaine's useful thought was: *In this heat?* Then—they were running straight at her—she was blown off the sidewalk by a blast of terror. She ran up onto a porch of a red house which in recent weeks she had come to love, and even now, shaking and sweating, she recited, as if to summon up protective magic by incantation, her customary form of response to the polyglot thing this house was: *Jesu, a Federal-period house with a Greek revival porch and a Queen*

Anne wing and God knows what kind of bay windows.

When she turned the men had run past and were gone. Her relief was mixed with a weird, bitter cognizance of not being at the center of things: they were not interested in her.

Leaning almost indolently against a fluted Ionian column, Elaine watched the trio run down Academy and around the corner. Then she looked toward home.

A heap of laundry on the sidewalk. No, it moved.

From somewhere in her viscera came a heat hotter than the hawk's, and she ran up the street.

Homer Plentagger looked up at her with cow eyes and said, "Get Merle out here."

Elaine had her movie reflex. Closed her eyes.

Seeing blackness she heard Homer Plentagger say, "Knife." Then he offered her a groan. "Merle," he said.

Opening her eyes, Elaine leaned down and placed the bunch of fresh mint on Homer Plentagger's chest. Even as she straightened up she wondered why she had done that. She whirled and ran.

Her hands were shaking so badly she dropped her keys on the floor as she fished them out of her purse. The key tip chattered all around the jagged slot in the lock, and when she had finally opened the door she ran all the way to the Plentaggers' in the back before she realized she had left her key ring hanging there in the front door lock. She tried to remember what she had seen in the street. It was as if she had forgotten a name, and in her struggle to recall it the name got jammed in a recess of her mind; the harder she tried to summon it back, the tighter the jam. She started to run out to the street to see what was out there, and at once it came back, all too clearly. She took her keys from the lock and said to herself, *You stupid cunt, you're wasting time.* She ran down the hall and punched the Plentaggers' bell.

Merle Plentagger looked cool and crisp as fresh Bibb lettuce at the heart of the head.

"Your husband's been hurt. In the street."

She was pointing like an idiot at the front door, which had just banged shut on its spring.

"Mother of God," Mrs. Plentagger said. "They got him."

"I think he's dying." Then at once: "No. No. I have no way of knowing that."

"Where is he?"

"Just down the sidewalk."

Mrs. Plentagger stepped back to open the apartment door wider, and she gestured to Elaine to go in. "Call the police. Get an ambulance." And she was gone.

Elaine had a hard time finding the phone. It was in the bedroom. The apartment was so clean, it looked sick. The dust ruffles of the bedspreads were like evening gowns waltzing. The officer at the police emergency number sounded as if he would fall asleep. She said, "I saw three men, they knifed him." Many questions. Her voice woggled. She became frantic. She shouted, "*Do* something, stupid!"

"Hold your horses, lady. We got a procedure."

Afterward she felt herself pulled back out into the street. Where had all the people come from? A big crowd in a silent circle, doing nothing. Elaine, saying, "Excuse me, excuse me," pushed her way to the center. Merle Plentagger was kneeling. Her chartreuse slacks were covered with blood. She had loosened Homer's tie and collar.

"They're coming," Elaine said, and then she realized she was looking at the first dead person she had ever seen.

She became aware that the hawk was diving.

She pushed into the crowd, ducking down, so the plunging talons would not find her. When she broke out of the circle she walked away with a staggering dignity as if to declare she was not the sort of person who liked to suck on sensation. The hot day had turned cold. Her abdomen chittered with the chill like a loose jaw. She went up her stairs two at a time. When she had shut the walnut door she leaned her forehead against it. After a few seconds she sprang away from it, bolted to the kitchen, swept up her straight chair there, carried it to the door, and wedged it aslant with its back tight under the door handle, so that even if Death knew how to pick locks, he would not be able to open the door. She was not ready for him.

Chapter 21

M ACABOY bolts out of his bed in his baggy pajama
bottoms and does a few dance steps. It is ten minutes to six;
he's a bit later than usual this morning, but he can accept his
delinquency as a mere blip in his image on the tube of fate.
He brims over. He has work to do. He is going to start a new
door. The sun promises beyond the Georgian buildings on
Park. Good! He sets water to boil, puts coffee grounds in his
Chemex. Eats a soft peach with soshing and slucking noises.
Flips on his radio. Zowie: Grateful Dead at five fifty-five a.m.!
He walks out of the pajama pants and pulls on boxer shorts
and jeans. Now a guy on the radio is trying to make the news
sound new by emphasizing unimportant words and mis-
pronouncing famous names. Macaboy doesn't particularly listen. Sound to him is like oxygen: it is in the air, he needs it,
he is not aware of the processes by which he takes it in and
burns it with his body. He fries three eggs. Grills some white
bread in the egg butter. In the midst of the sizzling he is
suddenly sharply listening. A name has been mentioned that
he has not really heard, and then, as a familiar word will
sometimes jump out at him from the expanse of a newspaper
page, he clearly hears a phrase which leaps into his ears and
revs up his metabolism: ". . . of 32 Academy Street." He can't

make out what happened to whom. "Police *are* looking into *a* possible underworld revenge motive. The victim had a record *of* arrests *on* gambling *and* numbers charges." Macaboy dives for the phone, then realizes he can't call her just after six in the morning. Now he doesn't trust his hands to work wood. He oils tools.

At eight thirty he goes around to Greenhouse's on Chapel Street and buys the morning *Journal Courier*. It is all over the front page.

He waits until nine to call. No answer.

He calls three more times during the day. No answer.

Twelve hours after he shot up out of bed good old Macaboy is in a state.

He has passed the time between the phone calls by looking at the pictures in her album. It is almost like going to the movies. The best films tell their stories by indirection, and here, in a series of crude stills, a kind of plot is offered for deduction. A baby girl, perhaps twenty months old, stands foursquare in a pinafore, her hair cut in a bob, with bangs; she is holding a stuffed koala bear by a leg at an odd angle, out away from her body; her underlip is pushed slightly forward, and Macaboy sees in the wide eyes a certain stubbornness—this child is on the verge of being spoiled by love. (The picture was taken, Macaboy figures, in the time of Truman. He sees a subliminal shadow photo, a cut from the film *Point of Order*, of Senator Joseph McCarthy holding up some papers: "I have here in my hand . . .") On another page—he skips—she is four or five, straddling her father's shoulders; they are at a beach, in bathing suits; she has coiled her pudgy arms around her father's forehead, making him an odd royal crown; above that, her face is ecstatic; he looks a bit hectic and blurred, as if he has had a few beers, needed them, and what leaps forward from this picture is the abyss that lies between the child's innocence, her absolute trust in the wis-

dom of her father and the hospitality of the world, and, on
the other hand, the father's knowledge, his effort to pretend,
for her sake, his look of a hangover, his realization that he
must salvage something somehow. It is a heartbreaking picture, taken in the time of decline of the Korean War. (Macaboy's shadow snap: the President of the United States pushing his putter at a golf ball on a green on the White House
lawn.) And this is a picture of two girls of about ten, with
arms around each other; one is not interesting to Macaboy, a
gamin, dirty-faced and pretentious, he feels, in her tomboy-
ishness; the other fascinates him—trying to imitate her
raunchy friend, to keep up; hair long, free, and straight, cos-
tume also straight; she has done her best to soil her clothes
but has not quite succeeded; a begging look in the eyes, but
the mouth quite firm and full: an odd impression, which the
viewer gets but the girl herself obviously does not have, that
she is more durable than the toughie beside her because she
seems to have calmly accepted, as the other has not, her
endowments: the Ten Commandments, Girl Scout's honor,
cheaters weepers, honest sweat, don't tattle. (Shadow picture:
John F. Kennedy, at the long table in the Cabinet Room,
with C.I.A. reps and staff, ordering the Bay of Pigs, his hand
raised in that decisive chopping gesture of his.) The mother
does not appear for several pages, but here she is, with a long-
wristed girl of about thirteen; they are posing in front of a
fortuneteller's tent in a traveling carnival, a rickety-looking
ferris wheel looming like a huge clock in the background; the
mother looking at the daughter with a manufacturer's self-
centered pride, bitterness however at some undefined loss
playing hide-and-seek around the lips, a prudish lift to the
sharp chin; the daughter not yet rebellious, meek, conscious
of being the cynosure, desperately trying to conform to maga-
zine definitions of what she should be; Macaboy can almost
hear the accepted kid words of the time coming out of that
eager little mouth: *def*initely, you know, cool, cram it. (Lee
Harvey Oswald seen from the rear, in the window of the

Dallas Book Depository, slowly moving the tip of his 6.5-mm
Italian carbine as the first of the cortege below comes into the
telescopic sight ring.) In *this* picture she must be in college,
she is standing in front of a crimped-up VW bug with an
idiot in an Esso grease monkey's shirt who is making ten-year-
old faces at the camera; she is wearing a Mexican serape, her
brassy stance tells that she has come out from the mothball
world of that father and mother; the face is a woman's, she
has had beneficial orgasms; yet there are glints of nostalgic
obedience that flash off the teeth bared by saying cheese, and
all the forced gaiety in the world cannot hide the inner cen-
trifuge, the flying id-bits, the feeling that big bones are pulling out of their sockets, ribs are afloat, the tower of vertebrae
totters—this is not a chick with a sense of her own integrity.
(Picture behind the picture: Lyndon Johnson in the Oval
Office, ordering McNamara to go to Saigon to report that
everything is indeed just as it looks from Washington.) Now
this is a damn good-looking young city woman, all pulled
together and very unhappy, standing alone on a stoop of a
house that can't be far from Rittenhouse Square, holding her
big sloppy canvas purse out away from her body, as if it were
a koala bear; an escapee from one kind of middle class into
another; in denim uniform; tucks of sensitivity around the
cheeks and mouth which belie the overall look of cool in-
difference; burning intensity shooting out from under a relaxed brow; an unutterable scream trapped in her beautiful,
easy throat. (Macaboy looks for a long, long time at this
photograph, seeing in haze behind it another: Richard Nixon
talking to reporters after his defeat in California, with sweat
on his upper lip, saying he will never again run for elective
office, saying in flat, expressionless tones, the unctuous
resonance of the duckbill nose in his voice tinged with bitterness, "You won't have Nixon to kick around any more.")
And *this* picture shows

＊　　＊

THIS time she answers.

"Where have you been? I've been trying to reach you all day."

"I have a job."

"A job? What doing?"

"Lampson. Mean anything?"

"Those crazy six-shooters—*you*? You're contributing to crime in the streets, you know that, don't you?"

"Yep, and pulling a paycheck."

"Hey, what's all this about a croaker that lived in your house?"

"Oh, God, Eddie, I was the last person he spoke to before he died."

Chapter 22

O<small>FF</small> its hinges, on its side, the door seems like a wounded creature.

Macaboy is installing a Stanloc. The door is out in the hall, set up in the metal work-brace. He is cutting a mortise for the new deadbolt above that of the present knob lock. It is Saturday morning. It is still hot. He has his shirt off. He is taking his time—he has all day; all night, too, for that matter. He has paused now, with chisel and mallet in hand, and they are speaking in low voices, leaning toward each other, their faces close together above the walnut leaf. Fear, like eyewash, has made her pupils glisten. He is so happy, he is on the edge of yodeling.

"You had Syndicate downstairs?"

"I sure didn't know any of *that*. He had this respectable cover, salesman for pest sprays—for gardens, you know, and house plants? He was supposed to be looking out for me while the Calovattos are away. Now I wonder about *them*—a Sicilian connection?"

Macaboy makes goggle eyes. He aligns the chisel. His taps with the mallet are gingerly, the bites of the straight chisel tooth are skin-thin.

She tells how the police kept her downtown, questioning

her, till after midnight. One of the pair that drove her down
was a fatherly old poop who was in the army of blueshirts in
her apartment the night it was broken into. He asked a lot of
questions in the squad car, apparently just out of curiosity—
wanted to know about the victim, said he'd arrested him as a
numbers bagman eight or nine years back. Elaine says this
was the first she'd heard of Plentagger's record; it scared her
almost more than the murder itself. It dawned on her then
why the ski masks on the hottest day of June: this was not a
five-buck mugging.

Macaboy watches her face for aspects of the story he has
read in the album. Yes, he sees the spark of stubbornness in
the eyes. The afterlife of trust. Innocence, or its later counterfeit. The mouth is soft, it has the expressive mobility of a
small child's mouth; the underlip pushes forward now and
then to remind that this small child was an only child. He
sees the contradictions, the stacked kindling. He thinks of
this woman as a lamination of sheets of developed film: the
incomplete person grinning on her father's shoulders beams
through the sensitive face of the good-looking woman on the
Philadelphia steps who looks with level gaze through the face
of this morning's anxious murder witness.

The cops wanted her to try to remember the colors of the
knitted ski caps. Pukey colors of what kind of a colorblind
manufacturer. How could a sane knitter design those awful
naked-larva golds and rotten-apple russets and pond-scum
greens to fly down over the purity of a Vermont snowfall?
The running men had featureless heads that reminded
Elaine, she says, of when her mother used to mend socks over
a darning egg.

"I admire your courage."

"Courage! I was spastic with fear."

"You did what you could to help him. Courage is a mutant
of fear. That was one of the things that turned me off in the
Movement. So many of the big talkers were cowards because
they'd never learned how to be afraid."

"Were you ever afraid?"

"I don't mean anxiety. I mean fear of real danger."

"Were you ever afraid? You seem kind of oblivious to me."

"I've never been tested. I don't really know. I was pretty scared in Chicago in 'sixty-eight. But not so much afraid of the cops—they split my head, that was bad—but my fear was more abstract: fear of the future, maybe. I don't really know about myself yet."

"My father drank quite a lot," she says. "He wasn't an alcoholic, just Irish."

"You use the past tense."

"He died three years ago. After he died I began to turn into him."

"You don't drink that much."

"I don't mean that. I don't mean I turned into a man, either—I never wanted to kiss my elbow. I mean that what happens so often—you know, when a child loses the parent of the opposite sex, the child becomes more and more like that parent in the months after the death: that happened to me. I grew into his unpredictability. I couldn't take anything seriously, a big mix of generosity and self-interest, a lot of horse-laughs, smartass answers, keep 'em guessing." The look in her eye now wavers, drifts into that of the believing kid on the hungover man's shoulders. "He collected restaurant menus. It only counted if he had actually eaten something in a place. Or maybe a drink would count, a gin would count. He papered the walls of our downstairs game room with them. He'd glue them on the wall and varnish over them. Everyone who went down there had to take a tour of the eateries of the civilized world with him. He'd point out how prices had gone up and up. He'd grab a person by the arm and he'd say, 'Look at this one! Imperial Hotel. I got me an R-and-R leave from Okinawa after the surrender. We went to these mixed baths, you know, the Slope women right in there with nothing on—.' And he'd take off on a wild story right in front of mother."

She breaks it. God, she's crying. Macaboy bends intently over his chiseling.

"I don't want to ever die!" she says with great passion.

Macaboy's hand is shaking. He makes a bad cut. "Shit," he says.

She apparently thinks this is aimed at her weakness. "I'm sorry," she says.

"No," he says. "My hand slipped."

"HE looked up at me," she says, "and he was calm, right? Like he was thinking of taking a nap after lunch. And he said, 'Get Merle.' You know something? I was jealous of her. This guy showed up at my door one night, practically exposing himself, in his bathrobe, he was a reptile, turned me all the way off—something really male-hormone and sexy about him, though. His pretext was, he wanted me to cut the volume on my stereo. But about the jealousy, it wasn't connected with him at all. It was the way he said it. 'Get Merle out here.' I wanted to be that important to someone—anyone —man or woman. It was like she and she alone could keep him awake from that nap. That made me so jealous. I guess she didn't get there in time."

"He was a gone goose anyway."

"I delayed. I got rattled. I was the reason she didn't get there on time."

"Look, Mzz Quinlan, that's kook talk."

MACABOY inserts the lock assembly in the mortise to see how it fits. Not too bad. He had been afraid for a minute there that he'd lost his touch. He breaks out whistling. A slice of *Salome*. John the Baptist is locked up in Herod's cistern; Salomé is warming up for the veil number. Herod: *"Salome,*

Salome, tanz für mich, ich bitte dich." Macaboy is so wound
up he makes Richard Strauss sound like Johann Strauss
dressed up as a cardinal bird.

T HE police kept asking me, did the perpetrators see me?
Did they get a good look at me? That question scared me
when I thought about it. I lay awake all night, and that
question started me imagining things. I couldn't tell if they
saw me. It was all a blur. They ran past me. I dodged up on
this porch. I could see the eyeholes in those sick ski masks.
But would they actually have noticed me? I mean I even
tried to imagine killing someone, then two seconds later,
running away, would I take a close gander at a witness? I
think I was a blur to *them.*"

"The Stanloc will protect you," Macaboy cheerfully says.

"Now that the guy is dead," Elaine says, "I've forgiven him
for the way he leered at me. First you forgive, when a person
is dead, and then you very quickly forget. I forgave my father
—for the way he drank, for everything. Then I began to forget things about him—that was quick, too. Was it because I'd
begun to absorb those things into me?"

Macaboy shrugs.

"No, Eddie," she says, "don't be so trivial. This is important to me. It's the afterlife. This thing on the sidewalk the
other day really started me thinking about my father living
in me."

"You going to take up the bottle?"

She looks as if she is about to be furious, but then she starts
to laugh. Macaboy joins in, and the laughter runs beyond its
evident cause. They laugh till they cry.

O N the mantel Elaine keeps a little clock with a polished
petrified-wood face—it speaks of time in two ways, about
minutes and ages. As its hour hand follows the course of the

sun over the city, stands up to noon and then begins the decline, the intensity in this pair, which makes them alternately as raucous as crows and as subdued and slow-motioned as starfish, remains undiminished. There are repeated bursts of father in Elaine; Macaboy stretches out two hours' normal routine into something almost motherly in its scope of patience and care. Elaine serves up sprigs of uncooked cauliflower, radishes cut into flowers, a bouquet of tongue-stinging cress, wedges of raw turnip, and some steamed brown rice—cold, but who cares? They drink beer together in friendship. With her talk of death and a continuum, Elaine has spread a kind of canopy of gravity over them, and they are so snug under it that they can laugh off anything. Macaboy explains the new lock to her. He holds the shell of it in his hands with great care, as if it were made of some substance infinitely delicate—wasp-nest paper, dried moth wings. But he talks of its steely power of denial. "Stanloc offered ten thousand bucks to anyone who could pick this baby. Guys from all over the world tried it. One copper, who boasted he could pick anything, up to and including the Queen of Sheba's vagina, worked on it two days and nights and then fainted. Most of your so-called pick-proof locks are a laugh: I saw a man pick one once that they had put out all this Madison Avenue wordage about its unpickability—he did it with a pipe cleaner! Not this Stanloc." He holds it up in front of his face, revolves it in his fingertips. "This is human safety." His gaze caresses the mechanism. He explains it to Elaine—she leans forward, intently watching—that she must operate it on each departure and entry; from the outside with a key, from within by turning this elliptical knob. His fingertip is on the knob, and it strikes him that he is at this moment printing on it the unique whorls of his right index finger; he is hit hard by the miraculousness of earth life. Forty billion unique patterns on the tips of fingers and thumbs in motion on earth at this instant of leaving his one smudged mark on Elaine's Stanloc. What are they all doing? Plucking harps, cleaning fish, adjusting the controls of atomic reactors; tracing partners' profiles from forehead to chin. In Macaboy's thoracic cavity the fist-sized muscle grasps and grasps and grasps. He sees the down on the cheek that is not more than ten inches away from his eyes, his lips. "I've got to get to work," he suddenly says, starting up from the straight chair. His movements are firm. He tests the seating. The tolerances are fine. As his sinews control splendid objects the flow between these two parties becomes wordless but is even more volatile than before. The lock is in place. He hangs the door. He tests the result and is excited. It is late in the day, and he insists he must leave. As the gap between door and frame narrows on his departure, the energy from his eyes funnels in toward hers like a draft. Then the door is closed.

Chapter 23

THE wind of that last look was still blowing on her face when she woke on Sunday morning. Her sleep had taken her to the floor of the sea, into such calm darkness as she had never swum through. She rolled out of bed, stood, raised her arms, and stretched, reaching for the summit of light so luxuriously that every muscle in her body seemed to yawn. Each mean chore she had let go since her first day of work now seemed a snap. She stripped her bed, made it with clean sheets, bundled her soiled clothes into a green canvas duffel bag, showered, put on a robe, fixed coffee and toast, started a Joni Mitchell record, ate, mopped the kitchen floor, dusted the Henrys and all else, emptied the wastebaskets, vacuumed the living room and bedroom floors—and all the while picked up energy, as if completions were honey and milk. She had dreaded these tasks, thinking herself lazy, resentful of anything smacking of charwoman's work, unwilling to be a servant even to herself; she was a little afraid she was becoming the sort of slophead who, through the perversity of her freedom, would very soon have cockroaches in her kitchen drawers. Not at all: her broom had wings. She was Clean Clara.

She thought of the motions of Eddie Macaboy's hands. She

saw in memory the two hands displaying the works of the lock, one hand cocked on its forearm to make a shelf, the deft fingers of the other giving the heavy item balance but also constantly playing, dancing, so that the metal itself began to seem to tremble and almost snort. "This is human safety." He was like a worshiper at an icon. He sat there and looked at you and waited, she thought, for you to say what you've been trying to say for years.

She was through with her housework by noon. She thought: I'll go to the laundromat, then I'll buy the Sunday *Times* and come back and read and do the puzzle. And maybe. Maybe there'll be a phone call.

She brushed her hair with a hundred strokes. She decided to put on her plum-colored corduroys. With a navy-blue tee shirt. Then, feeling Sundayish, she tied a silk scarf at her throat, French-workman style. She changed handbags, transferring wallet and cigarettes and Kleenex and odds and ends to her Pakistani velvet shoulder bag embroidered in gold, which she had bought in Paris. She picked up the duffel bag of laundry and started for the door.

As soon as she looked at the new lock she said out loud, "Oh, no!" She had no keys. Macaboy had gone off with that diesel-engine stare in his eyes and had forgotten to give her the keys.

Then she took another look. Hadn't he said that with each entry she would have to turn the oval button on the inside? She could remember his fingers resting on the button as he said it. He had used the word "elliptical." But there was no button. There was just the round flush fitting you had to put a key in—which he had said would be on the *outside*: she would have to lock it each time she went out, he'd said. He had turned the lock assembly in his hand to show her its two faces as he explained its working. Knob inside; keyhole outside.

She grasped the doorknob and turned it and pulled. The door was fast shut. She gave a frantic tug. No, it was not just stuck, it was *locked*.

The idiot! The idiot! He must have installed the lock backwards. How could he have done such a thing? He was so meticulous; she remembered what she had said to her mother: "He's so exact."

His forefinger rests lightly on the oval button. He is saying: It's not automatic, like a knob lock. You have to turn this button to lock it from this side.

She ran into her bedroom and looked up his number and picked up the receiver of the phone. Now this was odd—no dial tone. She clicked the receiver button again and again. In her left ear: black silence of interstellar space. Her next thought came burning like a shooting star out of that black infinity. She stood. She picked up the telephone housing and pulled it out into the room. A loose end of cut wire came away from the wall.

Chapter 24

M<small>ACABOY</small> has started the new door. This time, oak. Everything is tuning up. This door is going to be made with the assistance of the Beethoven quartets. The palpable dangers in working with oak are heaviness, dullness, an effect of banality and of nineteenth-century European bourgeois complacency. That haunting music, composed by a stone-deaf man, will demand bizarre harmonies of grain, narrow splines in the panels, integrity in the stiles but unexpected lightness in the rails. The last five quartets, crying out in anguished tones, never heard before or since, against the temporal and sensory limitations of human life, will force Macaboy to test to the utmost the stolidity of oak. Can he bring out the force of hidden incongruities? Can he, for example, make oak seem a bit racy, daring, even disreputable? He is much stimulated by the problems this lumber and this music set for him. He does not desecrate Beethoven now by whistling. His concentration is like a transmission of impulses through a glass rod. Yet his mind runs, as so often, in two channels at once, and besides challenging oakness he is thinking of Dandy Hartwohl.

In the smash-monogamy period Dandy Hartwohl ran through the female cadres of the Oregon collective like a dose of buckthorn bark. Carrying the full charge of a heavy-duty battery, Dandy (the nickname was ironic; he was a bucket of slops) sparked the women one by one. They were drawn to Dandy Hartwohl by more than the revolutionary call of the moment to share, and share alike, all progenitive resources. They lined up to get in the sack with Hartwohl. This was what Macaboy could neither understand nor like. The Hartwohl face was what an insurance adjuster would have had to write off as a "total." Acne had hit the dark skin with the impact of a load of buckshot; the black hair was tangled and hung down behind like an oriole's nest; the chin had a crooked cleft; the mouth sagged and gave off the stale stink of White Owl blunts, which he incessantly sucked at. Before joining the Movement he had been a sometime student at Grinnell. He had been attracted to protest by a choice presented one Thursday between a university sit-in (the issue: the right of male and female students to shit and take showers in the same bathroom) and a midterm test in English 20 (the topic: Jane Austen's *Emma*). In the Oregon group he had tried to attach himself to Macaboy as his best friend, but Macaboy found him a mean Joe. Dandy's father was a bitter, retired Army colonel who had been passed over for promotion, and Dandy, loudly repudiating the old soldier's values, unconsciously mimicked his transactions. And when Dandy Hartwohl fucked Sue Malden, whom Macaboy considered his girl despite the pressure for sexual socialism, and when Dandy Hartwohl began boasting publicly, in illustrated-lecture detail, about the sixteen orgasms he had caused her to have in a forty-five-minute span, Macaboy had felt a burst of uncomradely anger. He feels it again now. It does not help that he remembers Sue shouting that Dandy was a liar, a liar, a liar, and a male-chauvinist orgasm nut—she hadn't had sixteen orgasms, she had only had twelve.

The flurry of negative feelings rapidly passes. He remembers last evening. Macaboy holds up to window light the piece of oak—rather open-grained, almost feathery—that he has selected for the top rail. Yes, this piece will serve.

Chapter 25

SHE dropped the carcass of the telephone onto the
bed. The bedroom—wow—turning on an axis of the stretched-
out telephone wire? She hurried into the living room, hoping
to find stasis. After an unmeasured time she realized she was
standing there, scarf at throat, purse in hand, as if intending
to begin the departure all over again. *Courage is a mutant of
fear.* Once Aggie Bent tried to talk her into flying, like Peter
Pan, off the edge of her bed. *Flap! Flap! Harder!* Her wrists
moved when she was afraid. It seemed to her important to
figure out when he had cut the telephone wire. There had
always been someone to help, always. The day she threw out
all the stupid Gregtime hardware . . . Homer Plentagger
pounding on the ceiling below, probably with a broom handle, to protest the racket she had been making. That was it!
She ran to the wretched broom closet, and when she opened
the closet door she began to sneeze. Four, five, six katchoos in
a row. Her vision swam on the sudden Niagara in her nose.
She blew it on a paper towel and wondered if she was crying.
The broom. She grasped it from the closet, upended it, and
ran back in the living room. She had won the prize—standing
in her Girl Scout uniform on the mowed knoll of Brandy-
wine Hill, wagging the Morse Code with a signal flag, white

field with a red square at the center, to the observers on the town water tower—proud of her competence, her mind clicking like a ship's telegraph key: the sun behind her, the white and red of the flag mixed in a rippling pink passing back and forth above her eyes: *dot* right, *dash* left. She began to pound now on the floor: S O S: *dot-dot-dot dash-dash-dash dot-dot-dot*. While she pounded she dimly saw in her mind a man in a prison cell tapping on the wall in code to his fellow prisoners beyond it. *Darkness at Noon*. She had read it for Professor Muggsy Herwin and hated it in Comp Lit 32. But now she tried to recall the system the ex-Commissar—his name came to her, Rubashov—had used to simplify the signals; something about a "quadratic alphabet." She couldn't remember how it worked. She would just have to use numbers for letters. The message would have to be: LOCKED IN. L—she counted—the twelfth letter of the alphabet. She tapped deliberately twelve times. O—fifteenth. She tapped. As she paused before tapping an easy C she heard an answer from below. Merle was there! Elaine visualized her: still in her blood-stained slacks, she has dragged out a stepladder and is knocking on the ceiling, also with a broom handle—as if begging for help herself. She would have to wait to do the C till Merle had stopped and could hear. Or should she start all over again? What if Merle had deciphered the L, O—and thought she was tapping L-O-V-E? Something about the knocking below confused her, then made her feel self-conscious, then made her feel deeply foolish. The pounding sounded exactly like Homer's that Sunday. It had the quality of the buzzing of a bee. Impatient. Dangerous. The pounding was a snarl, its message: STOP. Did Merle think Elaine was on something— tapping out a high? Keeping time to the Grand Funk Railroad? Merle was a widow of two days; blood on her pants. There was a terrible rage in her pounding. Then it ceased. Elaine sagged on the floor and let the broom down. There was no doubt that she was crying.

*   *

*H*e went to the bathroom. They had been talking about the scene on the sidewalk. Macaboy asked, "May I have the courtesy of the house?" "My God," she said, "my Dad used to use that expression." That was how she remembered. That must have been when.

SHE threw open the southwest corner window, where she so often sat and looked at the world. She was not sure what she was going to do. She knew she could not scream. What was more, she did not now feel the need to scream; her fear had plummeted all the way to her Atlantic rift; the surface was calm. Her face felt hot—she wondered: was she blushing because Merle Plentagger thought her a noisy kid with all that pounding? Through the narrow gap in the buildings she saw the slice of urban renewal, on Court Street; at this morning hour the mall was empty. No! A fat lady came into view. Her huge legs gave her a knock-kneed, floating walk, and with each step forward she seemed to kick her tiny feet in an outward arc, almost as if she were skating. Elaine let out a timorous "Help!" The big lady skated along. "*Help!*" Her thin cries made Elaine feel, even in terror, a burning self-consciousness; she was a singing mouse. With five more dainty outward swoops of her model feet the fat lady glided out of sight. Elaine swam in an age of fear that no one would ever pass through that gap again. Then a girl came from the right, in blue jeans and a tee shirt with some sort of silkscreen design on the front. Elaine shouted as loud as she could. The girl heard *something*. Her eyeline swiveled like a dim, unsteady flashlight beam probing a misty night. The girl's face, turning vaguely for a moment toward Elaine, was as blank as the heel of a loaf of Wonder Bread. She did not break her pace; the dull beam swung away; she walked on out of view.

So much time passed in the empty street that Elaine's sense of alarm went out of whack: she hardly knew what she should be most afraid of. At last a stout, swarthy, gray-haired man in dark trousers and a white shirt—he looked like one of the Italian senior citizens who played bocce on the school grounds—walked into the opening. "Hey!" Elaine shouted. "Hey, mister!" The man stopped and seemed to search for the source of the sound but did not find her. The gap out to the street was narrow; the buildings must have been playing catch with her shouts. Louder: "Hey, I'm locked in!" The old lion in the street canted his head and stared around. *"Locked in!"* Perhaps, like so many of the very old men in the neighborhood, this one could barely understand English. He shook his head with a dark frown of alien disapproval. Elaine felt like a whore calling out from a street crib. The man turned and went on. Then no one. No one. No one. A tall young man walked hastily left to right. Jesus, he looked like Macaboy out of his coverall! *The company wants. . . .* Was her fear playing tricks on her inner eye? Elaine suddenly felt the mad whale in her rushing up from the deeps to breach all its tons out in the air. It *couldn't* be Macaboy at this hour. Her fear was condensed like propellant gas in a sealed can. Her next outcry—to no one in sight—blasted out full and strong and then cracked and went up in a ridiculous squeak. She was mortified in blank space. Then she thought: *That old man knew very well where the sound came from. He chose not to look at me.* She took a breath and was able to scream. For the first time in her life her throat opened froglike and she screamed. There was no one in the street.

SHE launched her confusion in her rocker. Maybe she would try pounding on the floor again later. Maybe she wouldn't need to, maybe Merle could hear her heart crashing in its cage. The motion of the waves under the chair gradually lulled her. That had been a twenty-four-year scream she had finally been able to let out. What if the myriad bits of the scream could have been unscrambled into coherence, as in one of those phone calls across an ocean? *O Aggie, why did I want your influence? Daddy, lift me up! You're crushing me, Greg, you're going to drive my ass through the mattress. Mom, don't contaminate me with your negative charge, against against against in the name of "love." What made you turn my button, Macaboy? I have been waiting so long! . . .*

SHE thought—how much later?—she might have a snack. When she opened the fridge she learned from her liver and lights that a snack would not be enough. She was famished. She made a peanut-butter-and-grape-jelly sandwich and ate a tubful of yoghurt and seven stalks of celery and drank a Tab from a can. Then she put a stack of gospel on the record player, watered her strawberry begonia, which was parched, and sat down again. There was no use standing up.

SHE felt a dopey haze settling over her. Not exactly sleepiness. Something more like—she had to face it—full-bellied torpor. She tried to worry about not staying scared but gave up. A voice in her said something always came along. Her father often said that. "Calm down, Evvy," he said to her mother when she whirled back in from the car, babbling that the battery was dead, as if it were a relative. "Easy does it, old girl." Not with Mom it didn't. She sounded like a chain saw, or one of those model airplanes that hornet around in circles. Five minutes later he was out in the street with his thumb up, looking like a man leaving his bed and board for the clean womanless air of Colorado. But no. The *first vehicle* to come along is Slippery Zilroy's tow truck from the Chevron station, cruising around to snatch parking violators, and quicker than you can say Jackie Robinson there is a rental battery in the Plymouth and Pop is pouring himself a wallop of Old Crow and saying to Mom, "Something always comes along, old Ev." Sometimes he said the reason he drank was because he was so lucky.

NOTHING came along. Silence of the big world. Out the window the shadows were pulling themselves toward night. No music was going now. The amp of the record player was giving out a hot buzz. Once Elaine thought maybe she should canvass how much food she had, canned and in the cooler. She racked her brains and could not remember ever having read in the papers, or ever having heard on the evening news —even the local news, which was all arson and assaults and gory wrecks—a single case of a person starving to death because of being locked in. She took a nap.

SHE waked into a half-minute stretch of her limbs. It was dark out. She thought she would read a bit. Might as well start *Middlemarch* again. Time on her hands, a long book would help. There was a layer of fog on her fear. Hazily she thought she was due on *Middlemarch*: the last time she read it was during the worst of Greg—many blank pages in her mind. She didn't like Dorothea Brooke that much, there was something priggish about her, she was a woman who could have done with some fleas in her underpants—but Ladislaw! Will Ladislaw was the cock and balls she was waiting for. She lit some lights and found the book and sat down.

Miss Brooke had that kind of beauty which seems to be thrown into relief by poor dress. . . .

Chapter 26

Macaboy has left his tool box at home. As a result, the front tire of the bike is full of antigravity powder, and charging along Howe Street he rears up, like Evel Knievel doing wheelies on his motorcycle, and tears along for nearly half a block on his rear wheel, with the small front wheel up in the air, revolving slowly on its ball bearings. He settles down and rides no hands the rest of the way to the New China.

He has remembered her saying that she was big on Middle Kingdom chow; once while he was planing the door they discussed nuances, Peking versus Shanghai versus Shantung versus Szechuan. He likes hot Szechuan best; she prefers North Chinese. Macaboy's stomach is lined with goatskin, he likes hot Mexican better even than hot Chinese, he could eat a stack of tamales right this minute with four-hundred-degree-Fahrenheit red peppers on them awash in Tabasco sauce.

Locks up on a lamppost. Goes in. Orders gumlo wonton, lichee har kew, and wor shui gai, to go. And some rice. Drinks some green tea while he waits, and leans back, super-hyper-casual, like Emperor Huang-ti waiting for a report on the Inner Mongolian concubine situation from his head eunuch.

Then he is off again, laying down circumferences of two

sizes on Elm. In the bicycle basket, three kraft paper boxes are wrapped to keep in the warmth, in yesterday's New Haven *Register*. As he rides he glances now and then at the bulge of newsprint on the top package. PEACE HOPES DASHED BY RUSSIAN OUTBURST. What he sees has to be the lower part of the front page. CITY MAN SHOT. MRS. IRVING STARTS TERM. A small headline attracts his attention, and he leans forward and reads, with a radar of peripheral vision tuned in for navigation:

DEMOCRATS CRY FOUL
OVER OFFICE BREAK-IN

WASHINGTON (AP). Disclosures that a salaried Nixon-campaign security expert was one of five men arrested during a break-in at the Democratic National headquarters has prompted Democratic accusations of "political espionage" and Republican denials of involvement. . . .

Nothing in the part of the story that shows tells *how* the break-in was accomplished, so Macaboy gets bored and drifts to the story next to it on the page.

VIENNA (UPI). Prof. Gerard Brauer got a standing ovation at the end of his lecture on the health hazards of sitting too long.

His audience consisted of prisoners serving long sentences at a prison in Stein, Austria.

H E picks the knob lock first. He feels, as a luxurious challenge, the pressure of time: the Chinese food, wrapped in the packet of human folly on the floor by the door, is cooling, cooling. A rhythmic creaking sound, which after a time he deciphers as outcries of uneven floorboards under the oscillating curves of the rocker, gives bite to his task of listening for—feeling with his fingertips for—the delicate engagement of the tumblers by the cylinder with the help of his picking rake. So she is flying over the moon on her time machine! O Macaboy, you lucky son of a bitch! Stay cool, man: The tiniest tremor in the fingers is a liberation movement for all the tumblers of the world *Tick. . . . Tick. . . .* Yes! The lock is sprung, the latch is withdrawn from the strike plate. Now—slowly—he turns the oval knob of the Stanloc. The door can be opened from either side.

The gumlo wonton may now be tepid, but Macaboy cannot resist the pleasure of waiting a little while, simply to savor this fact: *Mzz Elaine Quinlan, you are free.* All you have to do is walk to the door and open it and go anywhere you want.

Creak, creak, creak. *Ride a cock horse to Banbury Cross.* He cannot wait any longer. He enters.

"Do you have a double boiler?" he says.

"You bastard," she says.

SHE is seated on one side of the small enamel-topped table in the tiny kitchen. He is standing, dishing out the lichee har kew, now hot again, into a blue bowl, using one of her flat-bottomed Chinese porcelain spoons.

"Minute rice is barbaric," he says.

She is not talking.

"I brought you some chopsticks," he says. He pulls a pair, for her, sealed into cheap Hong Kong wax paper, from his breast pocket, and also produces an ivory pair of his own, carved with the magic gadgets of the Seven Immortals: the gourd, the fan, the flute, the crutch, the sword, the phoenix feather, the lotus blossom, and the tablet of admission to the Imperial court.

"I bought these from a guy who ripped them off from a very expensive whorehouse in Saigon," Macaboy says. "It was a place for lieutenant colonels and up. The guy was a tech-three. He had to steal a pair of silver maple leaves to get *in* the place."

She says nothing.

"I don't think you're impressed enough," Macaboy says.

Her eyes are fixed on a black chip out of the enamel of the tabletop.

"Look," he says, sounding peed off, and holding the chopsticks under her nose, and shaking them, "these things cost me three gold ducats and my left nut."

She is silent.

"What are you—in a coma? Hey, I'm good company. Cheer up, kid."

"Beautiful," she finally says, looking at the chopsticks. "I hope you choke on them."

THAT is the sum total of what he can get out of her. She is mute. He wolfs the food like the sheepdog in the dogfood commercial. She does not touch hers. "Eat, baby," he says. She sits with her hands in her lap. He finally takes her helpings and eats them, too.

"What about some decent tea?" Scraping the last grains of rice out of a bowl with his ivory chopsticks. "Let me pour that cold stuff out." He reaches for her cup.

Her eyes are up, now, and he sees in them a dangerous Irish radiation, like heat coming off rocks that have been in fire a long time. She says, "What do you want, anyway?"

"I told you. The company wants you to feel safe."

SHE has become Miss Outreach—friendly as an airline stewardess (on her day off). It is hard to tell what this bimbo will do next. Guessing her is like reading the weather map: the isobars don't mean much, you have to know what the jet stream is doing, you have to figure in temperature changes, and on top of everything else you have to assume that your forecast is wrong. They are still sitting at the small kitchen table. They have been talking about Angela Davis's acquittal, but suddenly now she says, "Hey, Eddie, my electric can opener is busted, would you look at it?"

"Sure. I mean . . ."

"You're so wizard with your hands. I've been watching your hands."

Hoo, he says to himself, this chick is going to steal my wallet right out of my back pocket. "Where is it?" he asks.

She gets up and looks for the broken machine in a cabinet. There it is, on a high shelf. Reaching up for it, one foot off the ground, that leg bent at the knee, she looks to Macaboy like one of those breastful mid-nineteenth-century French sculptures, *Deceived Virtue Consoled by Cupid*—the baby-kins god of love, touching fingertips with her, being here represented by a GE Universal E1UC11 Can Opener. She fetches it down. He starts puttering.

"I GOT into it," he says, "seven years ago, at the Camp Maplehurst convention. Up on the Michigan peninsula, near a place called Kewadin. It took me years to realize that that was just the moment when things went bad. See, we'd had these elder statesmen, Tom Hayden, Al Haber, Carl Oglesby, guys like that. They were, like, Eastern—Ann Arbor, anyway. White-shirt nonviolent. Brainy studs. They were articulate. At Camp Maplehurst this new bunch blows in—I was one of them, I guess, though I didn't realize it at the time. Sleeping bags. We paid twenty bucks for the whole convention, including food, if you could call it that. Peanut butter and jelly, horse-cock sandwiches. The new ones—let's see—O.K., blue work shirts. Desert boots. Mexican mustaches. You getting the picture? Sophomores from jerkwater colleges. The thing was, this new crowd didn't want to bother with history —all that Old Left and Liberal horseshit. Balls to theory. You know. It was put your body where your mouth is. It was morality, *values*. I had made a total and complete break with my mother and father, especially my father. The last thing in the world I would have done at that point was go home for Thanksgiving turkey. 'Blowin' in the Wind,' that was the sound of it. Smoked dope all the time. The Wobblies were the model, if anything—you know, those big old roughhouse guys out of a Western. We didn't believe in leadership—that was elitism. We had this endless debate whether to have a chairman ever. So finally we just picked guys at random to run the meetings—like, *Hey you run it today.* And it might be some total spaz. We had votes but we never counted them. Some guys wanted to draw up a paper, like the Port Huron Statement. Hell, no, that was bureaucracy, that would be sucking off the system. Well, I know now that was where— Kewadin was where—we lost the chance to . . . to . . . Did I tell you my father's been sick?"

"DID you bring your tools?"

"This is a social call, ma'am. Tools? For what?"

"To turn that goddam lock around the way it's supposed to be. That's what."

"Who's to say what's supposed to be?"

HE is talking like a popcorn popper, yet he cannot quite think what it is he wants to tell her. He feels as if he wanted to tell her *everything* in a hurry. About the time on the swimming raft at Madison when he felt such a surge of strength and pinned his father's shoulders to the cocomat— the pain like a memory of hunger in his upper arms afterward. About how Arden tricked him into breaking the Stallworths' window with the slingshot Arden had made from a beech fork and a strip from an inner tube, and Mr. Stallworth rushing out, in a rotary-mower rage, and Eddie's fear turning into laughter which seemed to have its tingling seat in his little balls, as they ran away—and how often over the years laughter has had in it a risible echo of those pursuing shoes: *Your father will hear about this.*

How can he tell her about his desire to be decent? His wish

is tenderized, pink, positively edible. But babbling away he
is, so to speak, wordless.

SHE is surly now. This has not turned out exactly as he
pictured it would. He rinses his ivory chopsticks under the
faucet, slips them into his shirt pocket, and says, "I got work
to do in the morning."

"You mean you're . . . Hey, Macaboy, aren't you going to
fix that lock?"

"Fix? You mean that new Stanloc? Nothing wrong with
that lock, Mzz Quinlan. Works supercalifragilistic."

She now stands, pale. "Hey, man, tomorrow is Monday."

" 'At's right."

If only he could touch his fingertips to her cheek—the fingertips that are able to feel that unbelievably delicate *tick*
when a tumbler finds its footing on the edge of the cylinder
as he works the picking rake *so* gently in—up—*there!* That
skin, that pinkish tegument of warmth and fresh milk and
estrogen, would surely give his fingertips the proper signal,
barely to be felt, at the moment of imminence.

But she is saying, "Jesus, Macaboy, I'll lose my job."

His face shines. "I'll call you in sick, first thing in the
morning."

"Who's going to believe *you?*"

"I don't know why, but people usually believe me, Elaine."

Chapter 27

I⊤ is still dark when Macaboy comes charging out of bed like a wide receiver on a quick cut for a jump pass. He was in such a hurry to have sweet dreams last night that he just took off his shoes and flaked and flipped the sleep switch, so now he runs into his shoes and shoots out the door and vaults into the saddle and vrooms in half light across to South Frontage and down to Sargent Drive and under I-91 and back along Long Wharf Drive, between the pike and the harbor. Not far from the wharf—a Coast Guard vessel is sinister in the dim promise, it has the iridescent skin of a sand shark—he dismounts, drops the bike, and sits in the grass and waits, looking across the water. There is new wine in the sky. The tide is high. An arrow is in his heart. Macaboy! Macaboy! This is going to be another day! So much is possible, so little has happened to you in all the years. Up jumps the yellow ball of energy, bouncing off the deck of last night, into the superstructure of stacks and ship funnels across the way in East Haven. It is so huge, so fast-rising, that you can't hide: the eye of heaven sees you, Macaboy, its direct look paints you a new color. The flat light of its stare brings out the truth on your face: *This man has made so many mistakes in a short life.*

*   *

Nine oh five.

"Lampson Gunsmithy. Good morning."

"Hello. Here Dr. Polazczychuk. Can you give a message to madam office supervisor? I'm calling for patient, she is not able to report work. What's—how you call it—can you handle?"

"Certainly, doctor. The name?"

"Miss Elaine Quinlan."

"Quinlan. I have to have the complaint."

"She is confined—yes?—wiz mild viral pneumonia. 'Summer flu,' yes? Highly contagious, huh, at this stage. These things spread like rumor, yes?"

"How long will she be out?"

"Hard to say. Depends how fast she improves. Huh. You write, 'Some days,' yes?"

"What did you say your name was, doctor?"

"Polazczychuk."

"Would you—"

"Certainly." Very fast: "P-o-l-a-z-c-z-y-c-h—"

"Excuse me . . . c-z-c- . . . ?"

"No . . . z-c-z- . . ."

"c-z- . . . did you say then c-h- . . . ? It's not that important, doctor. As long as—"

"Thank you. You'll pass message?"

"Right away, doctor."

He stops at George and Harry's. What he likes best for breakfast, if it's boughten, is a Western sandwich. He gets an enormous gooey Swedish, with the icing all stuck to the cellophane, for her. A pat of butter to go. A full quart of coffee.

* *

This time he turns the Stanloc knob and knocks three times.

A longish wait. Then: "Who is it?"

"Dr. Polazczychuk here. I have bring rectal zermometer." The accent is even thicker than it was on the phone.

"Go away, Macaboy."

He hears the creaking of floorboards moving away from the door.

"I brought breakfast."

He waits. Waits.

Creaking toward the door.

Still he waits.

Then he says, not very loud, "You know I can come in any time I want. Open up, baby."

From inside: "You are *such* a bastard." But then the door opens. She is wearing plum-colored corduroy slacks, a navy-blue tee shirt, and a small silk scarf tied French-workman style at the throat.

Macaboy does not say that he expected her to be in a nightgown. He says, "I watched the sunrise down on the harbor this morning."

"Knock off this game," she says. "It's getting on my nerves."

She is in a rotten humor. He takes the breakfast into the kitchen. The Chinese-food cartons, the bowls, the plates, the chopsticks—all are still on the kitchen table. The pans are in the sink. Macaboy starts cleaning up. She stands in the doorway.

He says there's no problem at Lampson's Gunsmithy; union contract, they probably won't even dock her pay, since they have a doctor's report.

He pours the coffee in a pot and sets it to heat. He dumps the cartons in the garbage pail. It needs emptying—where should it be left? She will not say. Out in the hall? No answer. He takes it to the door. She is right behind him. He stays in the doorway, leans to one side to put the container down. He turns and looks her in the eye. Two-twenty volts. Direct current.

"Get it over with," she says.

"Get what over with?"

"Whatever it is you have in mind."

"Breakfast," he says. "Come on, let's get it over with."

THIS morning she sips at her coffee. He sees the need in her lips, which are as sensitive as a snail's eye-stems. Gathered as if for kissing, they suck at the heat without touching the dark liquid, then the upper one moves down over the rim of the cup to the coffee's edge. The lip winces. The brew is hot. But he can see, in a minute, that the very first trickle has quickened her. Her color is getting better. She is testy. He admires her spirit.

"Everything was the way it was supposed to be. My older brother Arden went to Loomis, so I went to Loomis. Mother wouldn't get our clothes in Hartford, she went to New York. Rogers Peet—that was the right place for boys. I was destined for law school: you could go into law, business, politics. Law was the Protestant priesthood. I was the one who was chosen to be the priest. We wore jackets and ties at meals. You learned a certain way of talking. My mother's family had been in Avon since—well, since the beginning. Her people migrated to Hartford with Thomas Hooker and Roger Ludlow when they broke away from Massachusetts Bay. Hooker was the one who wrote: 'The foundation of authority lies in the consent of the people.' I had a sense of legacy dinned into me."

"Why do you keep spouting this stuff?"

"We're getting acquainted."

"That assumes mutual interest."

"Appetite comes with eating."

"I guess bulls can fly. It sure is raining bullshit around here."

"W<small>HAT</small> do you think you're proving?"

"This is not a proof."

"What is it—some kind of macho kink?"

"Not at all. Our company—"

"Don't *say* that again."

H<small>E</small> asks her questions, but she parries. It is as if she were taking the Fifth Amendment. She does not grant him the right to know. He has the strangest feeling that she is enjoying herself.

"Ruth Greenhelge told me you had a serious man."

"She did?"

"For a long time."

"Really?"

"She didn't like him. She called him a hairball. That's what a cat throws up, isn't it?"

"I wouldn't know. I'm an aleurophobe."

H<small>E</small> watches her breathe. As the air goes in, her breasts rise and move away from each other. The ribs of the weave of the thin tee shirt are stretched apart, as if there were an osmosis taking place through the fabric. She sucks life into her from all around her. Macaboy feels so light-headed that if she were to take a deep breath she might inhale him.

Then she breathes out. The fabric closes. The wastes that leave her body are tinctured with her fragrance. He imagines he can *see* her out-breath, as if the air were chilly. Her prickly quality hangs about her in a diffuse aureole of musk. Macaboy takes a deep, deep breath, trying to incorporate . . .

THE rule for Dandy Hartwohl was gratification. A woman was a guitar; her function was the expression of harmony through chords. Chords could only be made by plucking. The sooner—and the oftener—the better.

"How often do you play your dulcimer?"

"I suppose you're going to say I have lots of time to practice now."

"One thing my mother did give me was music. You know the early memories that stick in your mind? Mine is being down in the cave between the piano bench and the piano—it was an upright. My mother's feet pumping up and down on the pedals. And the vibrations all around you. I don't know if she played well. But those harmonies go into you like X-rays."

Elaine's eyes are downcast. She looks faintly puzzled.

"Remember Dandy Hartwohl I was telling you about? In our Oregon collective? Fifteen—twelve orgasms? All he cared about in music—and I guess in bed—was the beat. Tempo. To me, there is so much more. Pitch, volume, timbre—you know, the quality of the tone. Anyone can have a fast hard beat—but tone: that's something else. And memory, musical memory. To be able to recapture. I don't know."

She is looking at him now. He feels the arrow turn.

"Arden couldn't get at me when I was in there. So often when my father was angry my mother played the piano."

"I'LL put this Swedish in the refrigerator. You'll be hungry later."

"How long is this going on?"

"I'll bring you some supper tonight."

"But be fair, will you? I don't know what the ransom is."

Chapter 28

WHEN she was thirteen and her family lived on
Oak Street in Shaker Heights, a clan of raccoons staged a *fête
champêtre* in the Quinlan back yard every night. They overturned the garbage cans and spread a hoity picnic, and every
morning the yard looked like the fields of Woodstock after
the music was over. Her mother gave Elaine the job of cleaning up. Elaine was at the beginning of a turn toward the
Negative Principle; she struck; her mother, in a moment of
exhaustion, offered her a quarter a morning—and Elaine
knew she was on her way to winning. The raccoons drove her
father batty. Why did they choose *his* yard? They didn't upset
the neighbors' trash. They were true B & E artists. There was
simply nothing he could do to protect the garbage cans—
weights, locks, imprecations, dog repellents, a hinged wooden
enclosure. They feasted in his teeth. He bought a Havahart
Trap and baited it with peanut butter. The very first morning a baby raccoon smiled its tricky innocence through the
wire mesh. Both Mrs. Quinlan and Elaine wept. In a rage of
forced compassion her father opened the trap, and the fat
brown behind bounced away, trailing its striped bush, looking like the rear view of a frontier hat on a jaunty boy's head.

"It's a God damn juvenile court around here," her father said. "Right back out on the street."

The coffee cups were on the kitchen table. Her bed was a nightmare's-nest, still unmade. Lint gathered like coiled smoke in corners. She knew she should clean up. She had heard Justy rattling her garbage can in the hallway where Macaboy had put it, and this had brought the raccoons to mind. She sat rocking. She blamed herself for more than her laziness. She blamed herself for her self. How could she sit here smiling at her father's explosions? Like a passing puff of breeze a thought briefly stirred the leaves in her mind: She had much to confess. Her mortal sin, sloth, was simply a disguise under which all that was wrong in her lay dormant. For two days she had done nothing but loaf, and she was exhausted. It would have been so much easier if she had been afraid of Macaboy. Then she would have been canny, adrenaline would have given her speed, in desperation she would have tied sheets together and climbed out of her window. Instead she sat there thinking with half-hearted horniness of his glistening chest and arms when he had been shirtless the other day, installing the Stanloc. His strong hands played around her. Rock, rock, the masturbatory motion. She hadn't the energy to invest in an orgasm. There was no joy in her lust. Nor any guilt. She was bogged down in *Middlemarch*. Self-righteous Casaubon was too much for her. She was tired of all of her music. Her calathea in one of the cookie jars was brownish, but she could not stir to water it. The game shows on the tube made her want to throw up. She had no appetite. It was too much bother to be angry.

She dragged herself to her bed. She lay on her back, her eyes closed over a watery mind. Thoughts drifted there with barely effective swimming movements, like those of jellyfish.

MOVING toward light, she was aware of rapidity. She broke the surface and knew that the pace was in her heart. It flew. She expected fear but felt instead an air-conditioned excitement. Rivers of Coca-Cola ran through her veins. Had she just experienced—how? in a dream?—the rapture of the deeps? She thought: *Whatever this is, I have to give way to it, I have to let it happen to me.* It was at first an airiness, the body active in it—beautiful long ground strokes all the way to the base line, easy and relaxed, an awareness that the game was expressing itself through her; she was not the athlete but the instrument. The coolness in her yielded to a trembling flush. This was the first joy she had felt in months—perhaps ever—at least since childhood. *Light-years* away from any chemical high she had ever felt. Ride it! Ride it! Her heart was still pounding. She realized that she was in tears. Her weeping gave her the purest pleasure. Light was dispersed through the welling water in her eyes into its primary colors. At the place where blue and yellow fused there was a green of newest growth—Maytime. All the yearning of all the months was geysering out of her. She put her fingers to her eyelids to feel the tears, as if she could only trust a second sense to inform her of her good fortune, to confirm it. Something like a stream of milk, still warm from its source—it could only have been air—washed her throat and vitals. It was evidently not a dream, or the product of a dream. The good feeling seemed rooted in her. It clung. She tried to call up some skepticism, but it was stormed away by the speed of her pulse.

S<small>HE</small> was calmer, though her throat was still tight with joy. She thought of the motions of his hands.

W<small>ITHIN</small> a few minutes of her watering it, the calathea showed its gratitude, lifting its prodigal greens and yellows and reds and whites for her view. But it was the moss at the base of the jar that fascinated her. She held the jar in the afternoon light in the window. *This* was the green she had seen in that passing moment of brimming. She guessed she had never looked closely at moss—she had seen it always as a conglomerate texture, a velvet. Now she peered at its individuals. She began to feel her heart move again with a faster rhythm. All those incredibly delicate tufted stems lifting their tiny sexual organs to each other; some with pregnant capsules of spores on slender necks. For a second she thought she could feel in her cupped hands the excitation of the many lives.

Chapter 29

BALANCING a loaded tray on the tips of the fingers of his right hand, he squirts his left pointer at the doorbell button. This time he hears her come running. He turns the lock button. The door swings open. She gasps. "My God," she says, "what happened to you?"

Macaboy, grinning, does a parade-ground about-face, to show the back of his head; then he does another, and says, "Had my ears moved."

"Your ponytail—what a weird haircut! What have you done—joined the Marines?"

"I did it for you," he says.

"For me?"

"You thought I looked freaky."

"I did?"

"You gave me that impression."

She ignores this. Standing on tiptoes, she cases what's on the tray. "What did you bring? I'm famished."

"Spaghetti marinara. Manicotti. Melanzano alla parmigiana. Ensalata mista. From Leon's. I had to bribe them to let me take it out. For you, only the best."

HER eyes are different.

Having set the food on the stove and in the oven to heat,

he casually checks the refrigerator. No trace of that big, gooey Swedish. While he is cooling his nose, she says, "I'm low on groceries. Would you get me some junk in the morning? Here's a list."

All written down. Eggs. Mayo. O.J. A whole shopping cart-ful of etceteras. Quite a list.

Macaboy looks at her eyes. Something high-octane in her metabolism. He decides to take his foot off the accelerator; sees a sharp curve ahead with narrow shoulders.

"Actually," he says, "I had my hair cut for business reasons. If you played the game of associations, the average person's response to 'security' would be 'crewcut'—right? If you gave 'ponytail' you'd get something like 'addict,' huh?—next step is straight to 'burglar.' I couldn't afford that image."

She is an eating machine. Her face is flushed. She looks like Botticelli's *Madonna of the Pomegranate* with marinara sauce on her chin. She has both fists firing comestibles at lips which glisten with olive oil.

"In the end it's mental," he's saying. "There's no lock that can't be broken. You take a heavy padlock, tempered steel. You can't make a dent on it with a hacksaw. No use trying a blowtorch on it. O.K., so what's to do? You spray it with Freon, the stuff they use in air conditioners—you freeze the steel. Then *whammo*, with a sledge hammer. A thousand pieces. Literally. It like explodes."

She stops stoking. But it is only to salt the salad.

"These petty crooks don't pick locks. You wanted to install the Stanloc—it's pick-resistant. But believe me, Elaine, no-body picks a lock, except private dicks on the tube—and me. No, it's all breaking and entering. Ninety-nine times out of a hundred, it's a little pane of glass gets broken, and in. But who wants to live in a house without windows?"

She puts her fork down. Her eyes—ouch, the arrow turns, turns, turns. "What's wrong, Macaboy?" she says.

"My father's dying. My mother called this aft."

"Eddie."

He can't believe the emotion. Her tenderness has leaped straight out of her gluttony. He turns his head, face away, afraid he will blubber.

Then he gets his head together and says, "I have to go up to Avon tomorrow. Okvent said I could use his camper. I'll do your shopping first. Will you mind an evening without me coming?"

"Of course not," she says, putting her hand on his. This is the first time they have touched. "You have to go."

Chapter 30

His father's face is in profile. Strange: Macaboy can
see every thread of the plaid cotton collar below the chin, and
the khaki fisherman's hat above is so sharply in focus that he
can see the wavering golden net of reflected sun-ripples on
the shiny green underside of the duckbill visor—but the features in between are blurred. He knows there must be a big
nose. He can hear his mother say it, part proud, part mock-
ing, "It takes three generations for a Macaboy nose to ripen
to its full glory." He is a little uneasy, remembering: Was
"nose" a code word? But the nose is vague; Macaboy can see
right through it. There is a hot place where the eye belongs,
and a spiderweb, perhaps, of an outdoor man's wrinkles
around the eye. Pressing his eyelids shut for a moment, trying
to realize the half face, Macaboy tells himself that he hardly
knew his father. But he sees where they were standing that
day: on a bank of the Farmington River, near the railroad
trestle. It was May. They were fishing for shiners. Macaboy
was fourteen. His father was chewing his sentences all to
pieces, and Eddie couldn't make head or tail of what he was
trying to say. But in time the fragments began to make a
pattern. "Men and women . . . different gidgets . . . you may
have noticed." A gesture of the left hand—the right hand was
occupied with the rod—as if holding a half grapefruit, applied

first to the left chest, then to the right. "No one told me anything when I was your age. There was this thing that happened to me. At night there'd be this dream . . . about these gidgets—you know? . . . Wake up sticky . . . Scared me, Eddie-boy. For months, there, I was convinced I'd picked up a social disease . . . trip to Hartford . . . pay toilet. I had no one to talk to. Hardly knew my own father. Thought I ought to . . . to warn you." There on the riverbank enormous bubbles of joy and fear rode in Macaboy's throat, globes of croaking laughter struggling to get out. O glory, glory, hallelujah! His father was trying to tell him about sex. It was only five years too late. All the lurid details, up to and including putting it into sheep, into a grasping hand, into human mouths and bumholes, as well as into snatches—wet dreams, too—had been imparted to Macaboy when he was nine by his classmate Bemsley Caul, and a few months later Bem's older brother Hart, who was nineteen and had, according to Bem, put it into all those places and plenty of others, had taken to his bed, his left ball swollen up to the size of a dime-store tin globe of the world. Bem had taken Eddie to see the impressive mound of the sheet at Hart's groin, and Eddie had sworn a private vow never to put it anywhere at all. But Hart's marvel had turned out to be just a cruel case of the mumps. Macaboy and his father caught no fish that day. When the ordeal was over, they started home. They were halfway across the railway trestle when the four-fifteen whistled, close in. They climbed out to the side of the trestlework and hung on to the railings at the ends of the ties, and Macaboy felt wildly exultant. He was positive, as the train thundered past and the shaking of the trestle went to nine on the Richter scale, that his father was going to drop off and drown and float away like a log to Long Island Sound.

THE body was made in order to receive covering. The body is covered at all times. In the bath—he is four? five?—the washcloth floats over parts of the body. "Lie back, darling. I won't get soap in your eyes." Rough towel—all covered now.

"Look the other way, dear."

He was walking somewhere on a dirt road with Arden. Arden was holding his hand. Arden took him into a field, among tassels at Eddie's eye level which swayed and made a feathery film against the blue sky. Arden stripped one of the tassels and put half a dozen unripe kernels into Eddie's mouth, and he said, "Chew 'em. Don't swallow, Ed-boy. Just chew." The wheat became a kind of chewing gum. Sweetness came forth slowly from it. Arden took Eddie's hand again. They walked in the dust, both chewing. Eddie looked up at his brother's pale face and watched the sharp chin working under the huge nose. Arden looked so much like Father it was scary.

Sunday was the day when people drove around. Arden and he were on the porch playing the car game. Arden got traffic out from town, that Sunday, Eddie the cars driving in. They bet marbles. They knew the models cold. *Sample values: Falcon, Comet, one glassy; Lark, Tempest, two glassies; Biscayne, Belvedere, one onyx; Star Chief, LeSabre, two onyxes; New Yorker, Super 88, one biggie; Continental, Imperial, one cat's eye; any classic (Auburn, Cord, Packard, Duesenberg, etc.), two cat's-eyes; Stutz Bearcat (a man in Farmington owned one and drove past a couple of times a month), five onyxes or a steelie . . . .*
  A silver bullet shot past with bass utterances of exhaust. Eddie started up from his chair. "A Jag!" he shouted. "My God, Ard, I got an XKE!"

"Shit," Arden said. "Just because it was streamlined—"

"I know what I'm talking about."

"That was a lousy Sting Ray."

"Come *on,* Arden. How can you *say* that? It had those sort of underwater headlights. Much lower and longer than a Corvette."

Arden stood up and moved threateningly toward Eddie.

"Cheater!" Eddie shouted, loud enough for faraway ears.

Arden's upper teeth looked like a cowcatcher on a railroad engine. "Take it back," he said. "Say it was a Sting Ray."

"You can't make me lie," Eddie said.

Blizzard-pale, Arden reached down into Eddie's box of marbles and picked up a handful and threw them across the porch.

The rolling and bouncing sounds of marbles on wood had just begun when Eddie lowered his head, charged, and butted Arden in the stomach. Arden fell with a groan straight out of a Jonathan Edwards sermon. Eddie piled on.

"See here." Pop's voice.

Two words were enough. The boys untangled and stood up.

"Him and his goddam George Washington act," Arden said.

"Watch your cusswords, son," Pop said. "All right. Let's be seated. Now. Who's the plaintiff here?"

And so, as usual, they found themselves pitted in a trial. Due process would never persuade Arden that a Corvette was a Ferrari, but it hewed out a rough justice that Eddie could appreciate. Arden was sentenced to pick up the marbles.

Arden was on his hands and knees paying his debt to society with flashing eyes when Mom appeared in the porch doorway. "You sit there as a judge," she said to her husband, her eyes mirrors of her older son's, "and let these boys gamble on the Sabbath. No wonder they lose control."

Tʜᴇ bus let him out in front of Sewall's Pharmacy. He was a Lower Middler, and he had earned a long weekend. He was carrying his brown leather suitcase, in which he had packed home clothes: wool shirt, two sweaters, his L. L. Bean hiking boots. It was November. The elm trees on Route 44 were bare, their angular upper branches sharp Gothic writing against a blue paper sky. He ran up the front steps of the house. The fanlights over the green front door sparkled in the afternoon light. His mother came running into the hall and threw her arms around him. Over her shoulder in her grasp he faced the octavo Audubon of the white-headed eagle, *Haliaeetus leucocephalus,* with its claws cruelly sunk into the fat white underflank of a huge fish; he felt his mother's fingernails fluttering at the back of his neck. He pulled away and bolted down the hall to the door at the far right end, in which his father just then appeared. They hugged each other; Eddie held tight. The two men went into the study, leaving Eddie's mother standing alone in the hall; he was aware of her sweeping past the den door into the dining room and kitchen across the way. A fire was crackling in the study fireplace.

"Saw a buck and a doe and a fawn," Pop said, "right in the Hydes' orchard last evening. They came right in behind the houses for the windfalls."

"Sounds promising."

Eddie, who hated guns, was going to hunt with a bow and arrow. Pop had promised to hold his fire, whenever they saw a buck, until Eddie got off two arrows. Eddie had a fast draw from the quiver.

Pop moved over to his desk, picked up a pipe, bent down to light a pitchpine taper in the fire, and then stood sucking up a storm of blue smoke, his thick mouth like that of a horse lipping a sugar lump. He had on a hunter's red flannel shirt, and his khaki pants were tucked into old leather puttees that had belonged to *his* father in the First World War.

They swam side by side to the raft. Pop had a powerful crawl, the right arm curved more than the left, which flailed high on its swing forward as he lifted his face to breathe. On the raft they began horsing around. Macaboy felt his father's grip tighten—for what reason? The wet skins were slippery. There were some quick moves. They were down on the cocomat. They lay on their sides with their arms around each other, heaving like unhappy lovers. The raft was rocking in the waves. Macaboy's eyes were a few inches away from the reddish shoulder: those muscles were not kidding. He became very angry, but the anger was mixed with sadness and the beginnings of some kind of dread. Macaboy breathed the coarse smell of his father's assertion. He was on his back with a living weight like hopeless depression on his chest. He had a glimpse of the set jaw against the sky—could it be that his own face now had such a look of determined hatred as that? The wetness from the swim had become the hot salt wetness of bitter labor. His muscles ached. His whole body ached with a feverish melancholy that was like the strength-draining grippe of February. Then he felt such a stab of heat at the unfairness of everything that he could not keep himself from arching and hefting and tilting the sky on edge. He was on top then—it took some time to know it—his elbow hurt on the cocomat. He heard a strange man's voice in his own throat: "Had enough?"

It took a month for the raspberry on Macaboy's hip to heal. The mark is still there.

Chapter 31

SHE put on a house dress and cooked herself a real and entire dinner of the home sort, for the first time in months. Two broiled chicken thighs; a toy can of Le Sueur peas; a salad with wafers of red onion and rings of green pepper varnished with Wishbone dressing; toast; coffee. She had even thought to chill a pint carafe of Paul Masson chablis. Aretha Franklin on the stereo. A proper setting on her card table in the living room.

Her father had been loony for those BB-sized Le Sueur peas. There were some nights when he was in a zoomy mood, and she and her mother laughed and laughed with him. She remembered her mother telling the story of the Michigan basketball player named Ammon Lolly who took her to dance one night at the Black Angus. When he sat at the nightclub table he looked stunning in his blue suit. Tall as a yacht. But when he danced you could see he had no socks on. He was still growing, and the cuffs of his pants rode high, and his long ivory ankles flashed above his black shoes as he flung his legs around one of the stuffiest places in Cleveland. When the check came, he screamed. Mom did the scream with eyes like Daisy Mae's in *Li'l Abner*.

Mom must have been quite a dish when she was young.

There were many stories of avid wolves. Dad laughed them all off: a bunch of wackos. She was a virgin on his nuptial couch—that he could vouch for, and often did.

Elaine had the strangest feeling: that instead of sitting at her card table opposite the three soused Henrys, she was on an aisle seat on an American Airlines jet flying home from limbo. The stewardess has just brought her a second cup of coffee. Flying home from Gregsville. She knew now that Greg had been just an agent. His assignment: to give her a moratorium. She had been wondering whether he, too, hadn't locked her in, without her ever realizing it. For months. . . . The pilot comes up on the public address system: . . . *beginning our descent to Hopkins Airport, please fasten your seat belts and observe the no smoking sign.*

On the ground Dad is dead. She is deeply happy. Dad's laughter is in her. Plentagger made that possible. And she wonders: Will Macaboy's father enter into his son after he leaves life in Avon? Or can such immortality be claimed only for a parent of sex opposite to that of the vessel child? Perhaps that's not a rule. Macaboy has talked of his father with a prodigal's yearning and love. If the father dies into him, what will Macaboy then be like?

AFTER dinner she did the dishes and got her laundry together, bundled into one of her sheets. Macaboy would have to take it to the Koin-Kleen.

Or.

She saw it as she was stashing the soiled linen on top of the fridge.

She hears the doorbell and she runs to answer. She turns the doorknob and pulls open the walnut artifact—but not far: she swings it only about a foot. She gets a great lift from seeing Macaboy—that manic perfectionist—standing there in the hall with a tray balanced above his right shoulder on the fingertips of his right hand. (For he promised, last thing last night, that when he would get back from Avon on Wednesday he would bring her a Mexican dinner from Fat Taco's.) *They exchange a few words. She fills the door gap. Suddenly she darts a hand upward, the tray flips backward, he turns in surprise. She gives him a sharp crack in the balls. He doubles over. She runs past him down the stairs and out to the big world of law and order.*

She heard her old man laughing in her head. She undressed and went to bed and took off in a jet liner that swam underwater with sinuous movements of its fuselage.

Chapter 32

SHE heard the doorbell and ran to answer. She was wearing a work shirt and a pair of jeans. She turned the knob and pulled open the walnut artifact—but not far: she swung it only about a foot. She got a great lift from seeing Macaboy —that dear man!—standing there in the hall with a tray balanced above his right shoulder on the fingertips of his right hand.

"Are you O.K.?" she asked. "Your father—?"

"He'll *never* die," Macaboy said with a kind of vehemence: pride? bitterness?—she couldn't tell.

He made as if to move forward, but she filled the door gap.

"Was it a false alarm? Did your mother—"

"No. But the old cock's just unwilling to bow out."

Suddenly Elaine darted a hand upward to flip the tray.

Like a striking snake Macaboy's left hand shot across in front of him and batted her hand away before it could touch the tray. Then he reached and grasped her wrist—a Vise Grip wrench on a piece of soft copper tubing. This was the second time they had touched. "You crazy bitch!" he said. "Have you lost your mind?" His eyes had a forest fire in them. Letting go of her wrist he shifted his hand to high on her chest, spanning her collarbones, and pushed her roughly back into the room. The tray never veered by a millimeter from the horizontal.

He kicked his masterwork, the door, wide open. "What did you think you were doing?" he said. "It's pretty clear you don't feel very safe yet—huh?"

He was in a rage. Elaine began to laugh. Joy caused almost the same kind of gross fullness in her throat as the scream had, the other day. At the same time, she felt a wash of tenderness akin to what she had felt when she had looked closely at the moss. "My God!" she said. "You're human."

With a stiff back he kicked the door shut and said, "Get in the kitchen."

"Does a visit to your father always give you a need to pass the shit down the pecking order?"

"My father," he said in a suddenly quiet voice, "is a very gentle person. Very gentle."

She gave him a long stare, then turned and went into the kitchen. He followed with the tray.

EVERYTHING was as usual. She was sitting at the tiny kitchen table, and he was getting the dinner ready. He had lit the broiler to heat the tacos.

"I guess part of the reason for all that junk I went through in the sixties was that he hadn't prepared me for the changes. Black Muslims. Their rhetoric set my teeth on edge, and then I'd wonder: Am I a racist? The assassinations. Vietnam. I sit there with a 3-S, and my best friend at Reed freaks out *all the way* shooting up crystal. Everybody fucks everybody. When Pop told me bedtime stories he didn't have the right kind of imagination."

She was groping for reasons why she *hadn't* gone through all that junk in the sixties. She'd gone through junk, but not *that* junk. Greenhelge had seemed a big joke to her at

Bennington: so grim and angry. Elaine searched her own lack of anger—*it's like a vitamin deficiency.* Somewhere, perhaps, in the tension between her mother's predictability and her father's unpredictability lay a clue to the lack. She laughed off too much. She should be wildly angry at Macaboy right now. But.

The Mexican food made her feel hot on the top of her head. She had a place, abaft where the spooky fontanel had once been, as she thought of it, which broke into a sweat when she ate ginger or curry or hot pepper. She made Macaboy feel the place. This was the third time they touched (she counted the shove in the doorway as part of the second).

"You're a hot mama," Macaboy said.

"It takes the place of anger in my life," she said, for she was still wondering. "You know: I can say I'm a hothead."

"Cool," Macaboy said.

Elaine stood up. "You finished?"

He had just dried the last of the washed pots and had stashed it in the cabinet under the sink. He now did a matador's veronica, with the dishtowel as the cape, and said, "*Olé!* Guess so."

"Then sit down."

Obviously surprised at hearing the tone of voice of an elementary school principal, he obeyed.

She stepped toward the place where he had just been standing, pulled open a drawer, reached in, and came out with a long, pointed carving knife of steel that was not stainless—the old-fashioned cook's kind that really keeps an edge. She ran it six times down the slot of an Aladdin sharpener screwed to the doorframe to her right.

Then she faced Macaboy and, holding the knife stab-fashion, said, "And now we're finally going to get it over with."

"Get what over with? We already ate, remember?"

"I'm going to rape you."

"You're what?"

"You heard me."

Macaboy's face shone. He looked as if he'd been promised a chocolate-chip cone with a double dip. "That's a neat trick. How you going to get my thingumbob up?"

"You better wipe that smirk off your face, man. I'm serious."

"I read about that once," he said. "Three gals raped a sailor in a Pontiac coupe, in Jersey. They did it on a shoulder of the Jersey Turnpike, right near a speed-limit sign, remember? He brought charges. Said he was a virgin. Remember that case? I always wondered—how did it work? As I recall, he got a judgment. How the hell did that rape work?"

"Watch. I'll show you."

The fingers of her left hand were at the top button of her work shirt. They talk about the Women's Movement: this undulation, hinged on the fifth lumbar vertebra, where the hipbone connects to the backbone, was what she had now most subtly begun. Her right hand still held the knife high, its point aimed at Macaboy's comprehension. She unbuttoned the button and folded back three inches of shirt. Then, changeable as always, she kicked her left loafer all the way to the ceiling. She did a little one-shoe-on, one-shoe-off dance, as if going round the rim of a hillside meadow full of buttercups. The other loafer flew straight for Macaboy's head. He ducked. Her left hand went back to button work. This was slow labor; it seemed she usually used her other hand to button and unbutton shirts. She said not a word. She had no need of music; music would have been constricting, for hers was the erratic tidal tempo of the knowledge of power in conflict with trained modesty. The cleft deepened. After she diddled out the last button at her waist, she bent her left leg up and reached down behind and pulled off the sock. She threw it, like carelessly spilled salt, back over her left shoul-

der. Right sock next. Over the shoulder. She could see in
Macaboy's eyes that her work was not entirely in vain; laughter had pulled back and was hiding in the shadows, and something she had never seen before was out in front. That
something made her feel a blush climb slowly from her neck.
She flipped her rear shirttail out. But the left front shirttail
seemed to have a playful puppy in a growling grip on the
other end. She tugged and tugged. It came with a final *grrrr*,
and in one fluent move, like the shrug of a sincere person
who really does not know, her left breast and arm and shoulder and back came out from under cover. She switched the
knife to her left hand and backed away a little, as if it were
she, not he, who was threatened in clumsy-time. Then the
shirt was on the floor and he was again the one in danger; her
right hand took the knife back. She was made aware by the
pupils of Macaboy's eyes, which were shuttered down as if
bathed in brightest light, that every move of her body now
brought an answering shudder or lift of her breasts. She
pulled at the zipper of her jeans. Peeling her jeans with her
right hand upraised required motions too slow, and far too
serious in implication, to be called wiggles; Elaine felt as a
bird must feel in the moment before liftoff. She stepped in
her panties away from the puddle of denim on the floor. And
now, both hands raised, she gave herself for a very brief time
to primal motions that had, from history's beginning, roused
jaded Sultans and bone-weary bricklayers and tired husbands
and burlecue freaks to upper levels of interest. She stopped
that and lowered the point of the knife to the hem of 60%
polyester and 40% cotton at her right hip. With some help
from her left hand, and with great care—but keeping her eyes
on Macaboy's eyes—she pricked the knife between the edge of
the cloth and her skin, and flicked the blade outward. An
inch of the cloth was cut. Once more she raised her hands and
made the moves of delay and provocation. Then she cut
again and the cloth fell on her left thigh and slid down
her leg.

"Now, you crumb, is your thingumbob *up?* Or *isn't* it?"

"It is," he said.

"Stand up."

He did. It was.

She made a lunge for his fly with her left hand, still holding the knife for a strike with her right. "Get it out here," she said between clenched teeth.

"No," he said, and too easily grabbed her right wrist. "No."

She twisted back and forth and in her struggles mimicked, without necessarily meaning to, the motions of the seraglio that she had used to another purpose a few moments before, hips and breasts in fervent oscillations which showed how narrow, in the end, might be the gap between sexual aggression and self-defense.

"Drop the knife," he said.

She let it fall.

He released her wrist. "I don't want it this way. Put your clothes on."

Feeling suddenly naked, she covered her breasts with her forearms. Then she darted here and there picking up her clothes and went to her bedroom to dress. She was sort of laughing. She told herself the reason she wasn't angry was that Safe-T Securit-E Syst-M, with its "this way," had begun to make her feel supersafe.

Chapter 33

AT about ten the next morning there came a knock knock. What a dynamite surprise! A Swedish and a Western and coffee! She ran to comb her nut-brown hair, ran back to let him in. But when she pulled at the doorknob, it would not come away; its resistance ran up through her arm and shocked her shoulder.

"Who is it?"

"Quin! You all right?" Greenhelge's voice cut through the two-inch walnut like a Skilsaw.

"Greenie! What are you—"

"Let me in."

"I can't. I'm very infectious."

"Christ, Quin."

"Really. The doc said I wasn't to allow *anyone*."

"What is it?"

"Viral pneumonia. Bitch of a strain. One sneeze and—you may be catching it through the damn door."

"I tried to telephone."

"I've been temporarily disconnected."

"Just nothing when I called. No ring. No operator."

"I forgot to pay my bill."

"I called that Lampson company. They said you were out sick."

"Well. You see?"

"Let me in."

"I can't, Greenie. Honest. I have a temp. The doctor said I was poison, he wanted like a quarantine."

"What doctor?"

"It's a name like Polassichick."

"Spell it."

"P-o-l-a-s- . . . I'm not sure."

"*Quinnie.* You *called* him, didn't you?"

"I have it in the other room."

"Get it."

"Look, you're being nosy. Lay off. I don't feel so good."

"You sound damn funny. I'm—do you need anything? How do you get food?"

"Macaboy brings it and leaves it at the door."

"Do you want me to call the telephone company?"

"God damn it, Greenie. Leave me alone, will you? I'll get to my checkbook when I feel better."

FOUR FIFTEEN in the afternoon. The same knock knock.

"Who's there?"

"It's me. I called Macaboy when I got home this morning. I was worried. He confirmed what you said. He said you're improving."

"Bully for me."

"He spelled the doctor's name for me."

"You sure are a trusting friend. What does it take to make a believer out of you?"

"I couldn't find this Polak or Slovak or whatever he is in the phone book."

"He comes from Guilford."

"From Guilford he makes a house call in New Haven?"

"Greenie. My temperature is rising."

"The reason I came this time, Macaboy called me back this afternoon. He wanted me to give you a message. His father died. He has to go to Avon. He said he'd check in as soon as he gets back."

Chapter 34

By the second morning—it was raining cows and horses—her food was all gone. She had even eaten the little oval can of anchovy paste that Bottsy had given her as a house present, and now she was drinking glass after glass of water to put out the salt fires.

The sea in her was calm.

Macaboy had her album, and she didn't mind. She had figured it out. She remembered how, on the day he came to hang the door, she had talked about Venice, and he had nodded, as if to say, "Yes, I know." Sure. He had seen that picture of her in Piazza San Marco, sitting at the table in front of the restaurant next to the clock tower, on the sunny side of the square; she had asked the Dutchman at the next table to snap the photo. And the day Macaboy first picked the lock and found her throwing things away, and they'd talked, and she'd mentioned the Russian trip, and again that nod. She'd noticed it. Sure. He knew. She and Greg in Red Square with the mad onions of St. Basil's behind them. And another time: about body surfing on Nausset beach, and about those incredible Cape dunes. His eyes lit up that time, he didn't even have to nod. She'd seen what happened in his eyes. *That* picture showed her topless on the lip of the dune against the sky with the beach grass tickling her calves: that guy she'd met an hour before, the psychiatrist who'd walked way down the great beach, took the picture after they'd fucked in the sun, hidden in a crater of sand back in the dunes. For sure, Macaboy had her album. That meant she'd get it back, anyway.

THE Dutchman had admired her little Rollei 16S, and she had gone off with him to his room filled to the brim with grapy sunlight as if with *vino bianco,* in the hotel on the Grand Canal, the Gabrielli Sandwirth, with a shutterable window looking down on a zoo of red-and-black tugs, *Taurus, Ursus, Equus, Caper,* tethered along the bund out in front. They set fire to the afternoon on a huge, lumpy bed. He spoke little English. She remembered telling herself that following that sort of impulse was the natural thing. And those ten minutes on the Truro dunes—five minutes, the doc had a slight problem of *ejaculatio praecox*—the *idea* had been so wild!—three minutes' conversation with a good-looking stranger with salt spindrift frothing around the ankles and then a hurried climb into a moon landscape and immediate total knowledge: she had the hairy, sweet-mouthed man of science psychoanalyzed after four shoves of the well-developed walking muscles of his rear end. That Tufts student she got talking to on the Turbotrain to Boston; the professional baseball player—he was never going to make it big, he was on the Yankees' Syracuse farm team—who picked her up in the First Avenue bar called Rafe's; the man in Philly who looked exactly like her father—guilt-free incest; the unshaven hitchhiker on Route I-91 who had the price of a motel room in his pocket—the fillip of danger; and of course Greg, how many times at unexpected times?—two hundred seventy-seven spurs of startling moments? Always the giddy *idea* of spontaneity, the worked-up satisfaction in the head—and the slackness of the body, the orgasms as weak as sighs, the headaches afterward, the soreness for several days that she finally came to think of as her freedom tax.

Now she had cast all that off. She believed she had the newfound play and flexibility—and vulnerability—of a soft-shelled crab just after the shedding of the old hull. Her mind-trip the other day, coming up that way out of sleep onto a sparkling, crystalline terrain—all new—had been like a conversion. She had been yearning and striving for some such crisis, without quite being able to define it or name it, for so very long that she had reached a stage of utter exhaustion. For ages all her energy had gone into the hard work of being apathetic. Her readying had been months and months, years perhaps, of egoistic anxiety, until even that tight worry had grown weary, gone flabby. And then, the moment having been brought to ripeness in that limitless gel of futility, it had come: this explosive upsurge of ardent, tender possibility. She still mistrusted it.

Her windowful of rainy sky was growing dim. A second evening alone. Her hunger sang in her. The energy with which she had vibrated in all her waking hours since last Monday was thinned out now into an alertness in the mind. There was nothing left to do. She had dusted, washed, laundered, rocked, mulled. She was too excited, too full of her own fictions, to read. She floated in her fast.

She thought a great deal about the turning of the wheel —about Macaboy and his father; the generations. Her own father did a kind of soft-shoe dance at the edge of her speculations (she saw a shadow of her mother dialing a phone, dialing, dialing). She had understood that Macaboy had a powerful tie with the past, in his tangle with his father, the time-hold all the more intense now that the son had come so far back in from contempt, hot rancor. Even, she thought, if Macaboy had realized his revolution of "values" in the sixties, even if it had come out like a formulated plot, his new world would surely have had much of his father's in it. The old moral tickets were embedded in him, as determinant as spirals of DNA. His strong love now showed how deeply. Macaboy's big deal would only have been a translation. His father had fallen short; he wanted to go all the way. From the way Macaboy talked, she gathered that it was his father's failure to be completely himself that had enraged Macaboy.

Her hunger, and these thoughts, made her own father's existence in her more vivid to her than ever.

SHE was sitting in her chair when she saw sunlight lick the cross on the acute peak of the roof of the Lithuanians' church, St. Casimir's, up on Greene Street. Behind it—blue sky. Had she sat in her rocker all night, while a rutting wind mounted one cloud after another and chased it off to the south? She did not know. Time, too, had become a sort of emptiness.

THE noon siren farted across town. Elaine sat forward. For a flickering moment she wondered if Macaboy had abandoned her. Then it came to her that actually it was he, not she, who was being held captive by the walnut door. She settled back, began to rock.

IT was growing dark again. She managed to start the rocker swinging again. Her hunger was a thin humming contralto complaint in her ears, a monotone, not exactly a warning—a reminder, it seemed, of some other need.

*   *

Night. She was not really frightened. She thought she should go to her bed. She thought it and thought it.

Then she heard a real click and three firm knocks.

She was up in a rush, flying weak-kneed through a double darkness, of her room and her light-headedness.

She pulled the door open. Macaboy was a leaning tower. He had set a carton crammed with groceries down on the floor beside him. His face was side-lit by the bare forty-watt bulb in the hall. At what she saw, she lunged forward. Well-fed strength from some source surged into her consoling arms.

Chapter 35

I<small>N</small> the sidelight of the weak bulb in the hall the door
has a texture of dark shot silk. An oiling would bring this out
even more, he thinks. He puts the groceries down. Listens.
The rocker is not measuring her travels. He turns the Stanloc's oval knob. Raps the upper panel with triple authority:
father-mimic, fatherless son, doormaker. At the sound of swift
movement that he hears beyond the door he assembles the
appropriate facial expression of a man who has just taken on
the burden of his heritage. His deepest sadness, which he
doubts he can hide, is that he cannot yet get his hooks into
the emotion about his loss he considers his privilege and duty
to feel. Maybe this counterfeit sadness will show and tell
enough.

The beautiful slab of his work swings open and he sees at
first only a box of darkness, which astonishes him. Then out
of the black she comes bowling at him. She is in a jay-blue
housecoat. He catches an intimation of Victorian paleness,
glints of two sapphires; wings are outspread. She bangs into
him and straightens him to the perpendicular. He feels her
giving strength. Her body is hard and soft against his. Her
cheek is hot. "Darling, darling," he hears. "Are you all right?"

All right? He is aroused, while she clings. As when before?

Eiffel. Empire State in the trousers. He is as merry as a fox terrier. He wonders: Hey, is that my pecker, or Pop's?

"CAN I take a shower?"

"Be my guest."

"I came straight. I feel kind of raunchy."

"I'll get you a towel."

He waits in the living room. All the lights are now on; the room, he sees, is double-dusted, and every object is consciously placed. She has oiled the inside of the door: he feels her care as if it were of him, a backrub. She brings the towel. He thanks her and goes into her bedroom, and shuts the bedroom door.

He undresses, takes an admiring gander at his not quite detumescent selflet, goes into the bathroom, turns on the shower, and twists the shower head so the streams hit the shower curtain for maximum sound effect.

Then with ocelot speed he returns to the bedroom, gets a wire cutter, a knife, and a small roll of Scotch electric tape from his pants pockets, falls to his knees by the head of the bed, pulls the side table away from the wall, takes the phone from it, peels the wire ends with deft swipes of the cutter, matches the pairs, twists them firmly together, and tapes them up. Then he tucks everything back in place and goes and takes his shower.

"YOU must be some clean," she says, when he finally reappears.

"I was washing away my bad thoughts," he cheerfully says. "Ever since I got the news about Pop dying I've remembered dumb things he did."

"You're having a reaction."

"He always took my side against Mom."

"That seems dumb to you?"

"But, you see, it put her on a hell of a spot. One of the rules of her life was that you respected your husband's opinions. To my Mom, life's been a parlor game. It has like these rules. It's God's backgammon game—she's bonkers for backgammon. Life is a game of backgammon. You take what the dice give you, you make your moves, you move according to the rules. You *try* to win, but if you start losing you play a back game: you begin sacrificing stones right and left so as to build your defenses in your home table—where the other guy wants to do his winning. Since before I can remember she's been saying, 'No, Eddie. You may *not*. That's a rule. Remember?' So then just while she's saying it, along comes Pop and changes the rule, right in her face. He had her off balance three-quarters of the time."

"You're bound to have a reaction."

"You should have seen her at the funeral. She looked so relieved. I think she was glad he was finally out of her hair."

"Was your brother there?"

"Arden? Yeah. What a mess he is."

"How a mess?"

"He was coming on with this shit about 'Now that I'm the head of the family.' "

"Give yourself some time, Macaboy."

His words are bitter but his manner is blithe. His eyes are leaking ohms—his natural exuberance resisted by his sense of form. This is an aspect of the tension that makes him an artist in wood. He gives a blow-by-blow account of the funeral. It is a comic tale. The preacher, whom Macaboy's father always called Reverend Ichabod Crane, stood with his stalk neck sticking out of his backwards collar, intoning a gloomy eulogy that amounted to a slightly adulterated self-portrait. "Thank God they'd screwed down the lid of the coffin. Pop had to be laughing so hard under there that the mortician's makeup was cracking." His Mom was gawking around to see who had come. Arden looked as if he was adding figures—doing an inventory of the estate.

"I'm going to have some money," Macaboy says. "You know: Not enough and too much?"

THEY burn a roach, passing it back and forth, while Elaine gets dinner: a tuna-fish salad, with cut-up celery, and onion and olive slices, and tomato quarters, and halves of hard-boiled eggs. Macaboy's glittering eyes follow every move. Is she going to go to that drawer by the sink and pull out the carving knife? Something has surely shifted in her. Her moves are steady. She laughs in the right part of her throat. Her eyes are a buyer's eyes. He feels a stirring of the building trades in his pants.

She turns and says, "You were the undy-freak, weren't you?"

"The who-whaaa?"

"You're the one who broke in here—jimmied the door, you warned me about that gap, the old door—broke in here and got into my drawers: in both senses of the word. Right?"

He tokes and does a grassy ha-ha. Then with charming eyes he says, "It was part of the sales promotion for our company. You did place an order the next morning, after all—didn't you? It was a setup. I'm not really that freaky about intimate textiles."

"I know you're not," she amiably says.

"I'm a freak for what they cover," he says.

"Eat," she says, pushing the salad at him.

THEY both know what is going to happen. The death recedes. Their laughter is like kissing. He can feel his balls stirring. Her buoyancy exactly matches his. He is in a force field of her acceptance. The meal starts off like the eating scene from *Tom Jones*—every bite and lick and lip-shove is an erotic signal, appetite is a metaphor; but soon this tapers off, because the sense of perfect understanding causes extraordinary thoracic aches and a kind of lassitude. He puts his fork down.

Words have the tactile quality of foreplay.

"That's the best door I'll ever make."

"I oiled it."

"I noticed."

"You should see: the wood drinks the oil."

"I know. I've done it a hundred times."

Every short sentence has the texture of a groan. He who has talked so much about safety realizes only now, for the first time in his life, its sensual meaning. The wound he did not know he had is healing. The image of his father's gritted teeth fades. He sits at the kitchen table, reaches for her hand. Everything glides in his mind. Preparatory lubricants flow from his cock. He knows without having to touch that she is very wet, too; she is safe. He will not hurt her, he will not be heavy, she knows that. The utter safety of her most secret places will cause them to engulf and eagerly suck at his generosity, no matter how huge it is. This knowledge is the core of the promise of pleasure, and Macaboy has not the slightest fear that the promise may prove sweeter than the pleasure itself.

"O Macaboy," she says with a sigh. "You horse's ass."

He laughs and she laughs. He laughs at the woman's mourning at the idea of surrender. She laughs because she can crack the code of her own protest: It is he who is surrendering.

Their looks splice. No one has to speak. They rise and go together to the other room.

HER hair floats around her on the percale—the ivy hair of the Primavera. He is on his side, his head raised, his cheek on his hand, his forearm propped on its elbow. He is drinking in, by the dim indirection of the living room lights, her skinflush, the slight puffiness of her lips, her Libra eyes—in perfect poise. He tastes the hormones on a light kiss.

She turns her head from side to side, as if in persisting disbelief. "Jesus, Macaboy. Jesus. I had twelve orgasms."

He lies back and stares at the ceiling, and shifts a bit—the crown is a little uneasy on his head in this position. He believes her.

In sleep, too, she looks safe. Both hands together, in the flat attitude of prayer, are wedged under her left cheek. Her legs are drawn up. Her face still shows the swollen look of satiety and the trust of someone too young to know.

Carefully Macaboy slips out of bed. His clothes are all over the room. He stores up the memory of every move of their scrimmage. A laugh would waken her, he actually puts a hand to his throat to stop it. He dresses as he can.

In the living room he writes her a note. Then he turns out the lights, giving her the little that is left of total night.

He opens the door with great care, slips out, and quietly pulls it to. He looks at the oval knob of the Stanloc but does not turn it before he tiptoes down the hall toward dawn.

Chapter 36

AFTER lunch she went yet again to the walnut door—the twentieth time that day?—and placing her hands flat against its satiny surface she kissed it. "Hi, door," she said.

Once more she was in the throat of a two-day wait. His note had said he had to go back up to Avon to help his mother sort ducks and drakes, back Tuesday. And he had ended with: *Our service manager is grateful for your endorsement of our company product.* The signature: *Safe-T Securit-E Syst-M.*

"Hi, product," she said, patting the door. Then she doubted that the door was what he had meant.

She felt so loose she thought she might just melt down into a glob of oobleck. A zillion nerve-ends had come untied. She was too relaxed to be elated. She felt like an important number, rounded off to the nearest oh oh oh.

Late in the afternoon she noticed that she was walking a lot. Bedroom living room kitchen living room bedroom. . . . She still had the floating feeling of earlier in the day, she was paddling along the surface of a wish-fulfillment dream; but she began to feel a tidal current making up. She became aware, too, that in each room she was stopping to look out the window: at the high surge of the sycamores in the square, already brownish now in summer wilt; at the rusty jungle gym (had a child mercilessly grown up and drifted away?) in one of the Court Street backyards; at the funky outrageousness of the big Stick-Style house up on Greene Street, with its mazes of embroidered brick—just a glimpse of it was visible from her bedroom window—which Macaboy said had been built by a Jewish corset manufacturer in the 1870s and was now a Convent of the Daughters of the Holy Ghost. The sky was smoky, the sun was a yellow ashtray. She ate snacks. She walked again. She saw the evening sun go down. She rode at some fences in her rocker. Her thighs felt springy. She hugged herself. She was Elaine Quinlan.

SHE fumbled at the dials and caught a random part of *Patton* on the late show. The vast scale of the world seen through *this* window—the huge, endearing malevolence of George C. Scott, the terrain of a great war under a sky as encompassing as what a fish sees with eyes on the sides of its head—was weirdly reduced on the tiny screen of her Sony to a kind of peddler's sample of the whole truth. Huge and minuscule, the visible idea seemed to be that you could have life both ways. She felt confirmed in her sense of General Patton as a dangerous backlot bully, but she also saw in this swaggering puppet on her eight-inch viewer a person who might be construed as the right kind of red-blooded American, a true hero of the collective unconscious. Elaine was haunted as she watched by a memory of Scott as another kind of military man—General Buck Turgidson in *Dr. Strangelove* —and that sense of double exposure was immediately reinforced by the hemorrhoid-ointment commercial ("reduces stinging and itching in seconds") coming right on top of footage of exploding shells and tanks in flames. As she punched the off-knob she wondered: Could George C. Scott play Macaboy? He was a great actor, Scott. Could he catch the both ways of Macaboy? She remembered saying out loud in the recent past, "You were bound to have a reaction."

A CROWD running down a field off to the left, throwing heavy objects. She runs over, sensing that someone has been killed by the rocks thrown by the young people there. The rocks are half buried, grass has grown up around them. Elaine persuades the young people to help, turning up the stones. They find charred bones. A young man with a large airlines bag puts the bones in it as they are found. A pelvis is recognized. "That's old George C," the bagman says. Elaine, still kneeling by the stones, asked who did "it." A blond man in a coverall with some lettering on the back says he did. Then everyone is involved in pursuit. Elaine catches the blond man; holds him by the shoulders; and asks him: "Do you have an attorney? Do you? Do you? There has been a homicide. Do you understand? There has been a homicide." She shakes him.

Later money is being changed—four hands with dollar bills. From one of them the bill is taken, and two Kennedy half dollars are given in exchange.

For some reason this transaction is terrifying, and Elaine turns and runs all the way up to consciousness.

SHE slept till past noon. She awoke with a sense of levitation. Still in bed she stretched, and her feet seemed to float far, far from her upraised hands; her whole length shuddered in comfort. She remembered the dream; she did not usually keep her dreams. This one did not scare her now. Parts of it seemed comical.

She soared out of bed and fixed coffee.

* *

About three o'clock. A series of quick knocks.

Elaine scurried into her bedroom—hadn't expected him until evening—comb crackling in her hair—more banging—skidded to the door and pulled it open and flew into waiting arms.

Of Mary Calovatto.

"Oh, honey," Mrs. Calovatto said, pushing Elaine out of the hug. "How adorable! You missed me!"

Deep tan slicked with unguents to a Naugahyde finish. A bonnet and curlers.

Elaine whirled to face the door. "Just a *minute*," she said. "Tell me something. Did you turn this little button before you knocked?"

"What are you accusing me of? I don't fool around with people's hardware. You little bitch, you trying to say I was trying to pull a sneak?" She was off and running. "You don't have nothing—*nothing!*—that I'd pull a sneak for. I wouldn't *sneeze* at the hippie junk you got. Those flat-ass spoons. I don't like coming back from a first-class-accommodation holiday in the Caribbean islands and being accused of a two-bit break-in. I'm going to get Giulio out here—"

"Hold on," Elaine said, darting in at the door. "Be right back."

"Don't you try to call no cops," she heard over her shoulder. "Come back here! A person makes a friendly visit . . ." Elaine lost the rest to the shouting in her head.

She slipped and fell as she banked on the turn around the end of her bed. She crawled on her hands and knees, like a person dying of thirst in the desert, to the side table and plucked the phone off its cradle and banged the receiver to her ear.

Yes, there was a dial tone.

She stood up, hung up. She walked at a hostess pace to the

door and said, "I apologize, Mary. I've been jumpy. I've been having my period, and Justy—"

Mary Calovatto softened. "I *knew* that booger would give you conniptions."

"Come in and have some coffee."

"Oh, honey, I can't drink that tiger pee you make. Come in my kitchen."

"I have to stay here," Elaine said. "I'm waiting for a call."

"All right, I'll come in for just a second."

And for two hours Mary Calovatto told Elaine all about everything. There wasn't time for her to ask about Homer Plentagger; she had too much to tell. They hadn't gone to Cinnamon Bay to screw in the talcum sand. "I didn't need to take him there. When Giulio gets in that tropical air—look out!"

SHE dialed his number. No answer. Not back yet.

THE walnut door stood open. She walked back and forth in the living room, looking out into the hall.

"BOTTSY! How you doing?"

"My God, Quinlan, where've you been?"

"Right here."

"I tried to call you. I *needed* you."

"I was out of order. How's old what's his name—Pyotr Whoozevich?"

"That's why I needed you. I've had a *crise de mentalité*."

"A who?"

"I punted my fucking thesis."

"All that work?"

"I've decided to go to business school. Can you come over, Quinlan?"

"Not right this minute."

"I need you."

"I'M sorry I was such a louse, Greenie. I'm better now."

"Frankly, I was glad. The last thing I need—viral pneumonia. You know what I've got?"

"Greenie, you're going to have a logical baby!"

"No, ma'am. I've got crabs."

"You mean the Associate Professor of Linguistics and Logic gave you—?"

"Who else? You know me, Quinnie, I don't sleep around."

"I never had crabs. What are they exactly?"

"You have to shave down there. And put on this hideous purple stuff. You wouldn't believe the itchery. I had a bad moment there when you said you were sorry you'd been a louse. I thought you knew. I thought the bastard must have been lipping around. I thought you were taking a dig."

"How would I know? I've been—"

"Of course I've quit my job. . . ."

No one ever asks a certain type of person a single question.

"HI, Mom! What's new?"

"Lainie. So you're finally back from the dead."

"I've been working my ass off."

"Lainie, *please*. Sometimes I think you talk that way deliberately, to upset me. Your father used to do that."

"I know. I guess I'm like him. Listen, Mom, I called to tell you some news."

"Oh, dear. Is it bad?"

"Remember that man I told you about the last time we talked?"

"You're not in trouble again, are you, Elaine? You're not—?"

"He's going to move in with me."

"Darling child, you worry me so. Are you sure you want this?"

"You'd love him, Mom. He's had a short haircut. And he has lovely manners."

S HE tried his number several times.

T HE sidewalk was like a trampoline. The sun was on the lowest shelf of one of the longest days of the year. She bounced up Academy, away from the bloodstain. Two blue-jays were yakking in a sycamore, and Elaine thought: *No hawk for a long time now.* She bounced back and into Court Street, and flying past the gap in the buildings she looked up at her window—up there a girl was shouting, "Hey, I'm locked in," and Elaine just shrugged and bounced on. From here the window seemed rather small. She walked across the bridge over the railroad tracks and all the way past Orange and the Post Office to the Green. The world never changes— three churches, green Green grass, tall trees, geometry of paths, drunks on benches. Macaboy was a tricky character. He would play an elusive game. She would have to be strong, strong, strong. You don't just turn a key and unlock the whole bit. Look at Bottsy Feldman and Greenhelge: what fuckups. *Yes, Dad did teach me to swear, probably to annoy Mom.* Now that she had a job, she ought to be able to scramble around and get a better one. When she went off to

Bennington, Dad said, "Keep scrambling, sweetie." Macaboy
at least had one big edge on Greg: he could use his hands.
You could survive around anyone who could make a door
like that one. That door had patience in it, sweat, signs of
scruple, harmony, dignity, resistance; and also something
trompe l'oeil, deceptive, ominously coded and not safe. To
say nothing of a ferking blatant lock installed backwards. It
came through loud and clear that the dead father whom
Macaboy had loved so much was a failure in the eyes of both
father and son. Failure begets failure? What was she to think?
Must she think of the bad features of the door as husks of
seeds? What about the plateau of good feeling on which she
had found herself ever since her conversion, or whatever it
was? Had she got there by finding out that it is possible to
scramble? Sickness, paleness of the ego, money worries,
menopause, wrinkles, widow's loneliness, the approach of the
Great Cheater—later, later, alligator. Right now she had stuff
to take care of. Right now she had this difficult, shifty, double-
decked bastard Macaboy to scramble with—for—against. The
sunlight was creamy on the marble base of the memorial
flagpole as she walked past, starting homeward: it had the
names of lost men on it, and places of battles. One was
CHEMIN-DES-DAMES. She felt so great, and so unsure. Keep
scrambling, baby.

"THERE you are."

"Oh, good evening, Mzz Quinlan. Your telephone working
again?"

"My telephone is working again. How come you're home?
Last time you came straight here."

"You needed food last time."

"That's true. Hey, pal, just a matter of curiosity. When did
you first leave this here door unlocked?"

"Uh. Let me see. Ummmm. I guess it was time before
last."

"You mean all that first trip you took to Avon when I was so hungry—"

"I think it was then."

"You double-decked bastard. When you come over would you please bring your tools?"

"To fix the lock? Sure nuff. Pleasure. No charge."

"When are you coming?"

"Pretty soon. I have to make a phone call."

"Listen. I have a gorgeous idea. Do you want to hear it?"

"You are interested in a sequel?"

"That one's gorgeous, too. But no. Mine was different."

"Yes?"

"Why don't you move in here with me?"

"Oh hey I *like* that. That's ace. Beautiful. . . . I'd have to think about it a little bit. My workbenches . . ."

"I mean, sure, keep your shop over there. Just park your carcass here. See what I mean? You're such a good warmer-up of restaurant food—you know, to go—I need you around the house. Bottle washer, also. Also, I have in mind—"

"I'd have to think about it."

"Some response."

"Jeez, thanks, Mzz Quinlan. I mean I *like* it. Looks like I could really buy it, see. It's just that I have a very slow adjustment servo-mechanism. You know me well enough to know I'm cautious."

"I know this: you servo perfecto."

"Hey, I mean really. It's a beautiful idea. I'll think about it."

"Don't strain yourself. What time you reckon you'll get here?"

"I'd guess an hour. I can't make my call for like three-quarters of an hour. Then I'll be over."

"What is this big call, anyway?"

"I have this other door I have to sell."

"And then the Stanloc bit, huh? 'I brought you some chopsticks.' Huh?"

"No, Mzz Quinlan, you got me utterly totally completely wrong. Listen, Elaine, that part never happened before. It was because you—"

"You just watch your ass, Macaboy."

"I'd rather watch someone else's I know."

"That's better."

"I might bring a suitcase over while I'm at it. Some of my stuff."

"That's better. I'll have the door open."

Chapter 37

Something is not quite right about this oak door. Precisely the heaviness, the nineteenth-century *Weltschmerz,* that Macaboy feared and that Beethoven warned against—not (Beethoven) with cheerfulness but, rather, with a sense that only tragedy will serve—has somehow crept in. Macaboy counted on the resonance of oak for this door. Jove and Thor loved the oak tree. Indians ate acorns. When Andros demanded that the Connecticut colonists surrender their charter, they hid it in a hollow in an eight-hundred-year-old oak in Hartford. White oak, with glove-shaped leaves, some of which cling, though brown, right through the winter. Sturdy American tree. The most walked-on wood in the world; durable, workable, tight-textured. The fault does not lie with the wood. The judgment of the artisan has wavered somewhere.

Macaboy cannot unglue what he has glued.

He stops sanding. He cleans up the sawdust with his Hoover. He starts farting around with gadgetry, to pass the time—assembles a keyhole light, for which he has acquired the parts: a pencil flashlight, an automobile distributor dust cap, and a cast acrylic rod with a diameter of 250 millimeters. He boils up some water, heats the rod in it, bends it to a wide obtuse angle, fits it into the wire end of the dust cap, and sets the cap over the business end of the flashlight. What a nice little dingus!—no bigger than a busted ball-point pen, to throw light into trashed keyholes and messed-up lock barrels. He winks it on. Perfect! A little beam of light which goes around a bend.

He burrows in his closet and hauls out an ancient Gladstone bag, and he opens it out on the floor. He has never learned how to pack. Folding clothing is not one of his skills. He throws stuff in.

Then it is ten o'clock, suitable time for a call in the month of June.

"Is this Mzz Jennifer Ceeley?"

"Speaking. Who's this?"

"I'm calling for Safe-T Securit-E Syst-M, Incorporated. The company I represent wanted me to ask you a few questions about the security of your apartment."

"Security? You mean like insurance?"

"I mean like your personal safety, Mzz Ceeley. Like people breaking in."

"Oh, God, we had one of those. A woman right down the hall. Just last week."

"Exactly. Exactly."

A NOTE ABOUT THE AUTHOR

John Hersey was born in Tientsin, China, in 1914 and lived there until 1925, when his family returned to the United States. He studied at Yale University and at Clare College, Cambridge University. After serving for several months as secretary to Sinclair Lewis, he worked as a journalist and war correspondent. Since 1947 he has devoted his time mainly to fiction. From 1965 to 1970 he was Master of Pierson College at Yale, and he spent the following year as Writer-in-Residence at the American Academy in Rome. He has won the Pulitzer Prize, is a member of the American Academy of Arts and Letters, and is president of the Authors League of America. He now lives in New Haven, Connecticut, and teaches at Yale.

A NOTE ON THE TYPE

This book was set on the Linotype in a type face called Baskerville. The face is a facsimile reproduction of types cast from molds made for John Baskerville (1706–75) from his designs. The punches for the revived Linotype Baskerville were cut under the supervision of the English printer George W. Jones.

John Baskerville's original face was one of the forerunners of the type style known as "modern face" to printers—a "modern" of the period A.D. *1800.*

Composed by Maryland Linotype Composition Company, Baltimore, Maryland

Printed and bound by American Book-Stratford Press, Saddle Brook, New Jersey

Designed by Gwen Townsend